LILY BOWERS AND THE UNINVITED GUEST

JESS LOHMANN

CONTENTS

Cover design: Heather Brockman-Lee

Editors: Janell Robisch, Jennifer Navarre, Dr. Cindy Childress

First published in Germany on April 24, 2019: **World Day for Laboratory Animals** by Ethical Brand Marketing (Rel: 002/200625)

ISBN: 978-3-9820639-1-1

Dear Mom and Dad,
It was you who taught me to respect Mother Nature and all she takes care of. Thank you for that amazing gift I deeply and forever hold in my heart. May you both rest in peace with love in your hearts and light in your souls.
I love and miss you dearly.

To Michael and Leandra – my Lily – for your love, inspiration, and support. You are my world. I love you.

1

THE CHASE

Sprinting as fast as she could, Lily was barely able to draw air into her lungs. Her heart clenched tighter each time she tried to breathe.

Her life was in danger, but her long legs couldn't even carry her any faster. It was useless!

She swung her arms wildly in a failed attempt to gain more speed. She didn't dare turn around to see if he was still chasing her.

He was, though.

In fact, he was quickly gaining on her. Not only was he enormous, but he was also agile.

She swerved around the tree trunks like dragonflies speed over water, yet there was no way she could outrun him. But she was almost home. She could possibly make it! She prayed to make it to her front door.

Even though she knew this part of Reinhardswald, one of the largest German forests, better than her own basement at home, she didn't recognize anything. And that frightened her even more.

Where's the spruce tree? Where's that huge oak tree? Or the river? Or the sweet smells from the maple tree?

All the things she had cherished in her forest were gone. It still looked like a forest, but not her forest. It felt like a different forest in a different world, inhabited by different creatures. Scary and big creatures.

Lily felt him gaining on her and shrieked. His loud, labored pants made her even less hopeful of making it home.

Sweat ran down her forehead and met with her tears of utter fear.

She jumped as high as she could over a dead, fallen tree trunk that lay across the path. The toe of her shoe caught on a branch, and she fell hard on the ground.

"Owwwwww!" Lily had twisted her ankle.

There was nothing that could save her now.

Through the slits of her halfway-closed eyes, she watched saliva drip from his mouth onto her chin. She dared not lift her hand to wipe it away.

He hovered over her and opened his mouth wide, showing off his sharp teeth. His low growl interrupted the loud pounding of Lily's heavily beating heart.

Lily tried to move but squiggling did no good. The enormous being weighed at least double what she did. Any movement could cause him to harm her further.

She was trapped, or rather, paralyzed.

He bore his teeth again, growled like a rabid dog and leaned back, preparing to lunge at her.

Lily's entire body jerked.

Huh, what was that?

Lily looked around. It was dark and silent. And she was safe in her bed in her room.

That was a dream? Oh, thank goodness!

Lily inhaled deeply and wiped the sweat pearls from her

brows. Her hands were shaking, and her heart was beating like African tribal dance drums.

She wanted to get up but didn't because the pitch darkness was too foreboding. She crawled under the blanket and tried to fall back to sleep.

This is no use!

She was way too upset from the nightmare to sleep. She turned on her reading light and picked up the book she wanted to finish before school started back up in two days. She was only halfway through, so she may as well finish it now. There would be no time tomorrow because she was going to the amusement park with her parents—one of her favorite activities.

The letters and words on the page merged into fuzzy figures before her eyes. She couldn't concentrate on reading either. Abandoning the book, she curled up in a ball like a frightened pangolin with her eyes squeezed shut.

She squinted her eyes open just enough to read her clock. 5:24 a.m.

Ugh. Being too scared of the dark to get out of bed, when the alarm clock was going to ring in just an hour, was new. She had never felt this way before. Nor ever wanted to again.

"Briiiiiiing. Briiiiiiing. Briiiiiiing." She looked at the clock. 6:30 a.m. *Finally, thank YOU!*

While she had a fun day with her parents riding roller coasters, eating ice cream, and watching live shows, Lily kept remembering the image of that nightmarish body hovering over her. That was more frightening than the roller coaster and haunted house combined.

As soon as they returned home, she went to her room and laid down on her bed, still thinking of her dream.

Oh no. What if that was a sign that something's wrong? In my forest? What did that dream mean?

Now uneasy, she decided to make sure everything was alright. It was still daylight, so she asked her parents if she could go into the forest.

"Okay, but be home by 7:30 p.m. You know the rules, and besides, you have a big day ahead of you tomorrow!" said Lily's mom.

"Thanks, Mom!" She ran out the door so quickly that she didn't grab a jacket. As soon as she arrived in the thick of the woods, she stopped and breathed in deeply.

Ahhhhhhh, that's better. She immediately felt calm again. She was in her forest, her favorite place to be in the whole wide world.

She looked behind trees and even went off the path a bit, but nothing looked unusual. There was no scary creature. The dream was now just a memory of something that didn't happen.

Relieved, she went down to the river and sat on a big rock for a long time.

A dragonfly caught her attention. Her eyes followed as he zipped back and forth on the water's surface. Suddenly, he stopped in midair and turned toward her. He made a beeline straight at her, and they met nose-to-nose. Lily jumped at first but then froze as not to disturb her visitor. Her eyes were slightly crossed, so he backed up a bit as if to help them focus.

Lily smiled at his shimmering fluorescent blue beauty. She cautiously offered her finger as a landing spot. He flew to her finger, grabbed hold with his thin black prickly legs, and then crazily flapped his wings as if trying to lift her up.

Lily laughed and stood up just to amuse him, but then he flew off. Zip, zip, zip, he circled her a few times, then flew back to catching whatever was edible on the river's surface.

Amazing insects, those beautiful dragonflies. She remembered watching a documentary about their incredible hunting and flight abilities.

A cool breeze blew over her, and she wished she'd gotten her jacket. She rubbed her hands up and down the goose-bumps on her arms, then looked at her watch.

Uh oh, I'm late. Better head back home now!

Mud slushed under her rubber boots as she diligently followed the narrow path she had created from walking through the woods the same way. It meandered between the tree trunks like a snake's trail through sand.

Her phone beeped and broke her concentration.

"Lily! Last call! Time to come in and get ready for bed!" read her mom's text.

Now, she really had to go. The shadows of the trees loomed over her, but she didn't mind because this was her forest, where she spent her free time getting to know every puddle, tree root, and wildflower.

She trudged through the thin carpet of leaves, which had recently started twirling down from the monstrous oak and beech trees all around her.

Stopping dead in her tracks, she closed her big brown eyes, tilted her head back, and breathed deeply. Ah, the smell of sweet maple. This is where Marley, the only maple on the path, stood proudly.

She didn't name every tree in her forest, but there were a select few that she felt deserved a name. There was Ol' Eldridge, that big, lumpy oak that stood alone in the small clearing. And then there was Bernie, the birch that was shedding its bark one summer—a huge piece once fell from its trunk and hit Lily right on her head.

The sun was slowly saying goodbye to her through the branches overhead that almost carpeted the sky. To see more clearly, she turned on her cell phone's flashlight and continued along the path.

Tomorrow's a big day. A really big day. No more elementary school. No more dealing with crybabies in the first or second grades. Or loud, rowdy, gross boys. I can't wait to get to my new school.

Yes tomorrow, finally, she would start fifth grade at a new school. Learning in the same building with the twelfth graders would be weird. She was so scared and excited that her stomach felt like it was doing somersaults on a trampoline.

Don't be scared. She kicked a stick into the air. *Remember, it's never as bad as you think it's going to be.* That's what her mom said anyway. That it would be just like when they had moved from Colorado in the United States to Germany after Dad had gotten a new job. Before she knew it, she would have tons of friends again and forget that she was ever worried.

It'll be good. This new school will be really good. At some point, she was going to have to believe it.

Her elementary school teacher, Miss Flens, had been the best teacher ever, and Lily already missed her. *Will my new teacher be nice? Or will she be strict, like that one substitute, Mrs. What's-her-face? We were stuck with her for four months. Ugh! That would be horrible.*

Her head hanging low with her long bangs covering her eyes, Lily weaved back and forth through the trees, passing the small clearing that would soon be full of autumn colors. She expertly sidled down the slippery, muddy hill and swung around a big spruce tree. It towered over the flat rock where she sat down and wiggled into the opening she'd cut through the thick brushes, leading to her backyard.

Those bushes were all that lay between her house and her beautiful forest. They certainly weren't much protection from the wild boar who roamed at night, but she wasn't scared.

"As long as you don't get too close or threaten them, they won't hurt you. If one charges you because you're too close, move away at the last minute to confuse her, find a big stick to protect yourself, and a tree to climb—and call me to come get you," her mom had told her a few times. She also warned Lily not to be in the forest when it was dark.

Simple rules that Lily had never broken. Until tonight.

2

LILY'S NEW FRIEND

She just wasn't ready for the new school tomorrow. Feeling safe in her forest for as long as she could was worth breaking a rule just this once.

Not that she didn't feel safe at home. It was just that the forest offered her something many humans couldn't: quiet. And an entirely different world. A world of peace and nature. And pure beauty.

Lily found beauty in every living being. Even as a young girl, she was fascinated with small insects crawling on the ground or flying in the air. Or spiders creating their webs.

Most of all, she loved the sounds of the forest: the chirping, the rustling of the autumn leaves when they blew off the trees, the distant calls of the birds of prey. And when it was really still at night, she could sometimes hear a wolf's howl.

After being exterminated by hunters in the late 1800s, German forests were silenced, and the human fear of the wolf had dwindled. But now, thankfully, they were slowly starting to come back, and that made Lily's heart sing out loud.

Her dad always told her she was raised by a family of wolves because she spent all her free time in the woods.

Sometimes with a friend or her parents, but many times alone.

As soon as Lily walked in the door, she heard her mother sigh with relief, who immediately scolded, "I told you not to stay out so long. It's way too dangerous, Lily!"

"But it wasn't really dark yet. The forest isn't dangerous. But okay, I'm sorry, Mom. I just lost track of time."

"Losing track of time doesn't cut it! Next time you're late, I'm grounding you, do you understand?"

"Yes, Mom. I'm sorry." Lily put her head down.

Lily's dad was reading the paper in his chair, and he looked up and winked at her. She winked back and went upstairs to get ready for bed. Dad was always way calmer than Mom about stuff like this.

Later, her parents came upstairs to tuck her in.

"Mom, how did you feel before your first day of middle school?"

"As nervous as a cat in a carrier heading to the vet. But there really was no need to be nervous. My teachers and classmates were great, and it was a valuable experience. I'm sure you'll have a lot of fun and get so much out of it. Now, get to sleep, it's late. Goodnight, dear."

"Goodnight, Mom. Goodnight, Dad. I love you both."

"We love you too. Sleep well." Her parents turned off the light and left her bedroom.

Not really sure what her mom meant with the valuable experience part, Lily laid on her back, looking up at the glowing stars taped on her ceiling.

"Please let my teachers and classmates be nice. Please, I'll do anything!" she whispered to anyone out there who may have been listening.

After a while, she drifted off to sleep.

Suddenly, a loud noise awoke her.

"Aaaaaooooooh!" A high-pitched howl pierced Lily's ears.

Startled, she shook her head, trying to make it go away, but she heard it again, closer this time—too close! Her eyes flew open. Her room was perfectly still. She shifted her gaze to the balcony door. *Is that a shadow?*

It moved quickly, and she pulled the blankets up over her head.

"Mom! Dad! Help!" she whimpered in a weak voice that remained muffled under her covers.

The dream she had the night before invaded her mind as small sweat beads formed on her forehead again.

Scriiitch. Scriiitch. Scriiitch. Lily uncovered one eye. The shadow was still there, this time moving slowly behind the white gauze of her curtains.

A high-pitched whine, almost too quiet to hear, drifted through the door and into her room. Before she realized what she was doing, the covers were off, her feet touched the thin carpet, and she scuffled toward the balcony door.

With one swift motion, she pulled back the curtains. She squinted through the glass, but it was too dark outside to see anything.

"Eek!" Lily stumbled backward. A huge dog-like face came into view. It was staring at her. Or at least she thought it was a dog, but it was bigger than any dog she'd ever seen.

As her fear increased with each second, so did her curiosity.

She slowly moved toward the window of the balcony door again.

Looking straight into the dog's pleading eyes, Lily felt a wave of sympathy and calmness flow through her body.

Instinctively, she carefully opened the door and whispered, "Here doggie, are you okay?" He took a few steps toward Lily behind the glass door.

He was no dog. He looked more like ... a wolf!

"Ack!" She quickly closed the door and the curtains; her heart jumped in her throat. Just as she took a breath to yell for her dad, the creature scratched on the door and let out a faint whimper.

Maybe it's hurt and needs help. I can't just leave it out there alone.

Lily peeked through the curtains. The animal cocked its head and looked at her with big, sad, lonely eyes.

But he looks so sweet.

"Are you hurt?" Lily asked through the glass door.

"Yes, my tail got stuck in a trap. I was lucky I did not step in it," the animal replied. His voice reminded her of her dad's soothing voice.

"Come on in." Lily opened the door without thinking twice. "Let me take a look at it."

The animal gingerly walked into Lily's room, and she crossed the room to flip on the big light. When she turned back around, she gasped. "Oh my! You certainly are no dog! Are you a wolf? I've seen wolves before, but you're a lot bigger than they were."

"Yes, I am a wolf. A big one, but not a bad one," the wolf chuckled.

The enormous wolf was beautifully marked with black, brown, and beige fluffy hair. There was one single black vertical line on its forehead, champagne ears, and a white mouth highlighting long, dark whiskers. Brilliant mint-colored eyes studied her as the creature took long deep breaths through a flared, pitch-black snout.

I've never seen a more magnificent ...

Lily froze in mid-thought. Her thick eyebrows drew together. "Wait ... hold on a second ... you can ... talk?"

"Only with you," the wolf said.

Lily's knees felt like jelly as she stumbled to her bed. *This must be a dream.*

The wolf whimpered again, interrupting Lily's reverie.

She shook herself back into reality. "Oh, I'm so sorry, I

forgot about your tail. Please, lie down. I'll look at it."

Lily immediately checked his fluffy, brown tail. It wasn't broken, but there was a clear cut from the trap, and the wound needed to be cleaned.

"I think you'll be alright. Wait here. I'll be right back."

Knowing her parents would not approve of her uninvited guest, she knew she had to be very quiet. She tiptoed downstairs, past the living room and through the kitchen, to get the first aid kit from the pantry. Luckily, her parents didn't wake up.

When she came back, the wolf was lying down in the same exact spot.

After cleaning and bandaging the wound as best she could, she clapped her hands together. "There you go, as good as new!"

"Thank you," the wolf replied in a low tone and stood up. "I knew you would help me."

"Huh? How?"

"I know how much you love and care for animals."

"Well, that's true. But still, I could have screamed and hollered for my parents who could have hurt you. Or worse, killed you!"

"I knew you would not scream though."

"I wasn't so sure though. You really did frighten me." She paused. "Hey, are you a boy or girl?"

"I am a male."

"What's your name?"

"Alo. The mother of my family, Alpina, named me. It means 'Spiritual Guide.'"

"Nice to meet you, Alo, I'm Lily."

"I know." Alo bowed before her while lowering his head and bending his right paw underneath his chest.

"Really? How?" Lily sat on her bed.

"I have known you since you were a young child. I often watched you play in your backyard."

"I would've known that," Lily protested.

"One day, when you were carefully freeing a butterfly from a spider web, you spotted me."

"Hhhhmmm, I don't remember that at all!"

"You were very young and had just moved here. We stared at each other for quite a while, but as soon as you ran to get your father to tell him I was there, I scurried away. It was not time to meet you yet, and it certainly was not time to meet your father. But now, you are ten and old enough to understand."

"Understand what?" Lily leaned in, listening intently.

Alo paused. He continued in a low, quiet voice. "How to heal her."

"Who? I don't understand. Is someone sick?" Lily's mind was racing. "Why are you here anyway? How did you know I love and care for animals?" she asked without giving Alo time to answer. "Tell me, please, what is going on?"

"You will find out everything soon enough. Now, get some sleep. It is almost daylight, and you are going to have a big day tomorrow."

Before Lily could ask how he knew about tomorrow, Alo turned around, went outside, jumped off her balcony, and ran across the backyard.

Poking her head outside the door, she watched as he ducked through the hole in the bushes and disappeared into the dark woods.

Lily rubbed her eyes to make sure she didn't imagine the entire encounter. A cool breeze swept into her room, and she closed the door.

Crawling back into bed was easy. Falling back asleep was impossible.

What did Alo mean, "heal her"?

Lily struggled to calm down. As her thoughts finally faded, her head deeply sank into her pillow until she was finally asleep.

3

MEAN GIRLS AND ROWDY BOYS

Music suddenly blared from her alarm clock. Lily sat straight up in bed, a little spooked. The sun shone brightly through her curtains. Jumping out of her bed, she went to the balcony door and opened it.

She had a clear view of her backyard and her forest. There was no wildlife present, except for a few chickadees eating breakfast at the bird feeders around her garden. Their chirping was also the only sound she heard.

Was that another crazy dream? Seriously, what is going on?

She shook her head in disbelief. As she started to close the door, she noticed a tuft of hair hanging on the door frame.

She pulled it off and inspected it. It looked like the same hair from the wolf.

But that's insane! I couldn't have spoken to a wolf last night!

Shaking her head again, she started to get ready for the first day at her new school.

A nervous feeling crept up in her stomach. Feeling nauseous, she frantically ran toward her bedroom door to go to the bathroom and tripped over Ralph, her Marginated Tortoise.

He was Lily's only pet and often found clever ways to get out of his huge terrarium that took up one entire wall.

She loved how calm he was most of the time, but boy, could he make her laugh.

Her best moments with Ralph were when he devoured dandelions in the yard. Dandelions were his absolute favorite food, or at least that's what Lily thought because he groaned and rolled his eyes back when he chomped down on them. Then, when he'd eaten the last piece, he would whimper and look up at Lily with big, bright eyes, as if to say, "Feed me some more, I'm starving!"

"Ouch! Be careful, Lily, I am not quick enough to move out of your way!"

She froze in her tracks. *Now my tortoise is talking to me, too?*

"Yes, I can also talk, just like Alo," he said. "We all can actually, but only you can understand us."

"Well, I don't understand any of this. What is going on?" Lily sat down on her bed, too confused to feel nauseous anymore.

"I do not have time to explain everything to you right now. You have to go to school, but do not worry, you will be just fine," Ralph said.

"Lily, come on down, breakfast is ready," Lily's mom yelled from the bottom of the stairs.

Lily obeyed her mother and went downstairs as if in a trance.

"Ready for your big day?" her mom asked.

"Of course she is. She's been ready since the second grade. Right, Pumpkin?" Her dad chuckled.

"Err, uh, yeah, I'm ready. I just hope my teacher's nice." Lily slowly woke up from her coma.

"Well, we met her at the welcoming ceremony, and she seemed very nice," Lily's mom said.

"Mom, you say that about everyone." Lily rolled her eyes and looked at her dad, who nodded in agreement.

After breakfast, Lily got her stuff ready, kissed her parents goodbye, and walked to the bus stop. Her old elementary school was in walking distance, so this was her first time riding a bus to school.

Her two best buddies, Eva and Till, met her along the way. They had become friends in elementary school right after she moved to Germany.

"Oh wow, I love your 'do, Eva!" Lily complimented Eva's beautifully braided blond hair. All summer long, they practiced new braiding techniques from DIY videos on each other, and apparently Eva had mastered the technique on herself!

Lily let out a sigh of relief when she saw Till. Not only did his presence always calm her down, but he was also two years older, so he already knew everything about the new school.

"Oh yay! I'm SO excited!" Eva cried.

Till rolled his dark blue eyes, "Chill out, Eva, it's just a normal school with normal kids."

"That's what you think, Till." Eva turned to Lily. "Well, aren't you going to say anything?"

"Oh, I don't know. I'm a bit nervous and excited at the same time. I just hope our teacher's nice." Lily stepped onto the bus first and slid into a window seat.

Eva sat next to her, and Till took the seat in front of them and turned around to continue the conversation.

"Hi, Till. It's nice to see you again." A beautiful girl turned around, flipped her long, wavy auburn hair, and smiled widely at Till.

"Um, hi, Viktoria." Till's normally pale-white face turned bright red.

"Wow, who was that? Your girlfriend?" Eva chuckled.

"No, she's just a girl in my class, no big deal."

"Wait a minute, is that THE Viktoria Marc warned us

about?" Lily asked. Marc was a friend in their class who they often hung out with.

"What do you mean with 'warned?' Viktoria's a nice girl. To me anyway." Till shrugged his shoulders.

"Well, he said there was this one red-haired girl named Viktoria who was two years older and a bit of a bully. And that she was especially mean to girls in the 5ᵗʰ grade."

"He also said that we better not mess with her and to become invisible when she's around, remember?" Eva added.

"Thanks for the reminder!" Lily shook her head.

Become invisible. Yeah, right! Now how is that going to happen? I left my vanishing cream at home!

Familiar nausea curdled inside her belly as her throat felt as tight as a lemon being squeezed dry. She knew how mean girls could be. In first grade, she got a good taste of them, back when she got frequent tummy aches.

She remembered the time when she had found a quiet place to read. Then, Cora pointed and laughed at her, saying no one wanted to play with her during recess. Then there were the numerous times Susanne, a 4th grader, commanded her and her friends to take her plate up to the counter in the cafeteria, or else. And she couldn't forget the times Johanna stole her books and buried them in the sandbox. The last time she did that, Lily's math book was missing over the weekend, and she couldn't do her homework.

Some girls were bossy and mean, and some boys were loud and rowdy, which made her stomach turn all different ways. The doctor told her mom that there was nothing physically wrong with her, that it was all in her head. Her stomachaches stopped in the second grade after things settled down, but since this was her first year in the new school, she was now afraid the phantom tummy pains would return.

I'm ten now. I can handle this. Even catty girls and annoying boys. Lily took a deep breath.

They arrived at school. As she stepped off the bus, she tried to absorb the mass of older kids around her. Her elementary school only had about 100 students. Her new school had about 700, according to the brochure.

Right before she reached to open the door to the main entrance, three older girls cut her off, opened the door, and let it slam right in front of Lily's face.

"That's Viktoria in front, the one Marc warned us about. And those must be her groupies behind her. I guess we should stay away from all of them," Eva whispered.

Lily just looked at Eva and nodded in silent agreement. After all, the last thing Lily wanted was to get pushed around.

They opened the door and walked in.

Stale building air invaded Lily's nostrils. "Breathe in the good air, breathe out the bad," her grandpa used to say, but how in the world could she do this now? There WAS no good air.

Instead, she closed her eyes and envisioned herself standing near Marley, the sweet maple tree in her forest. Looking up toward the sky, she spread her arms out to each side and breathed in as deeply as she could.

Ahhhhh, much better.

Lily's eyes were still closed shut at school, but in her forest, they were wide open as she spun around and around with her arms spread out. Not being able to focus on anything, she just smiled as the wind blew in her face. The faster and faster she twirled, the more out of focus the forest became. It was one green blur now.

"Eh!" Lily jumped as the face of a strange old woman suddenly appeared right in front of her. Too close in front of her.

The first bell snapped Lily back into reality.

"What just happened?" Lily asked in a frightened tone.

"Are you okay? It looked like you were in another world," Till asked.

"Yeah, I'm fine. Sorry, I was just daydreaming."

"I gotta go that way. See you two later!" Till left Lily and Eva to go to a different part of the building.

"Come on, Eva, we better hurry up." They hastily moved through the halls and sped past the crowds of screaming kids to get to their classroom.

Lily walked in and noticed that she wasn't the only one who was nervous. No one was sitting still, and book bags were lying all over the floor.

Her stomach made another flip.

Please, Mrs. Whatever your name is, be nice.

Lily's teacher walked in briskly, turned to the class, looked up over her rounded spectacles on the tip of her nose, and seemed to attempt a forced smile. "Good morning everyone! It's nice to see you again. Find a seat and place your bags on the floor to the right of your desk."

Within seconds, everyone was sitting still and quiet.

"If you've already forgotten, my name is Mrs. Weinart, and I'm so excited to welcome you to your new school!"

"First on the agenda: roll call. Raise your hand when I call your name." One by one, she called out each student's name on her list. Everyone was there.

"Okay, glad that's over with. Right now, I'm going to give you a tour of the school. I want all of you to partner up with someone and walk in twos right behind me. Don't get out of line! There are too many classes walking around today, and I don't have the patience to play 'Hide and Seek.' Understood?"

After Mrs. Weinart gave the children a tour of the school, it was time for a short recess.

"Whew, she's kind of bossy, isn't she?" Lily whispered to Eva.

"Yeah, really. Her tight bun makes her look like a nun who has no fun." Eva laughed at her own rhyming win.

They walked over to Till, who was talking with his class-mates about soccer.

"Ugh, soccer. Let's go and play with them instead." Eva pointed to a small group of kids from their neighborhood.

On the way over to them, Lily jumped back as a small bird flew right past her head and landed on a nearby branch. "Have a nice day, Lily," the bird chirped.

"Thanks, you too," Lily chirped back.

Oh no, I completely forgot that I can talk to animals! Whew, glad no one noticed. I better be a bit more careful.

Eva walked up to the group and asked if they could play together, but Lily didn't want to play right now. They were fun friends to be around, but her thoughts were now on that wolf and this morning's conversation with Ralph.

I have to see that wolf again. What was his name again?

"Alo!" Lily said. "That was it!"

"What did you say?" Marc asked.

Lily's cheeks warmed. "Oh, nothing, I was just thinking out loud. What are you playing?"

Trying to look like she was having fun playing their game, she still couldn't get Alo off her mind.

"Lily, pay attention, it's your turn!" Eva yelled.

"Oh, sorry."

The bell rang, and Lily gratefully scurried back to her class-room. How could she concentrate on the game with images of talking animals dancing in her head?

4

THE MAGIC COIN

The rest of the morning flew by. After the lunch bell rang, Lily and Eva met Till in the hallway to go to the cafeteria together.

As they were standing in line, a group of rowdy boys from Lily's class tumbled into Lily, forcing her to bump into the girl in front of her, who lunged forward into the girl in front of her.

"Hey, watch out!" Lily shouted at the boys.

Her anxious heart pounded loudly as the girl in front of her quickly turned around. Lily's fist clutched in a tight ball. Startled, she jumped back into Till's broad chest. It was Viktoria.

Till stepped between the two girls. "Viktoria, it was an accident, some boys ran into her," he said.

"Well, okay. If you say so." Viktoria smiled at Till and turned back around. As she was mumbling something to a friend, Viktoria slowly turned around and shot Lily a nasty look.

Trembling, Lily turned to Till, "Thank you. I don't know what I would've done if you weren't here."

"It's alright, don't worry about it, she's not really mean."

"Wow, that look she gave you was not cool though," Eva whispered from behind.

Feeling nervous about the cafeteria incident, Lily was relieved the rest of the afternoon flew by, too.

On the bus ride back home, Lily thought about her not-so-nice teacher and Viktoria, who was also not so nice.

Tomorrow will be better, I hope.

As soon as Lily got home, she rushed inside the house, quickly said hi to her mom, and ran upstairs.

"Lily, come back down please, I want to hear about your day," her mom pleaded.

"It was great, Mom. I'll tell you and dad all about it during dinner. I gotta go into the woods now to see if the bird I helped yesterday is okay."

"What about homework?" Her mom yelled from the couch.

"Not on the first day, Mom," she yelled back from her room.

"What about Ralph's terrarium? Did you clean it?"

"Mom, I clean it every day. It's sparkling and Ralph is happy. Can I go now, just for a short time, please?"

"Okay, but be home by six!"

"Thanks, Mom, you're the best!"

Before her mom could reply, Lily ran downstairs, out the back door, and toward the bush that led into her forest.

She walked briskly, trying not to step on the little black beetles with blue, shimmery bellies that seemed to be everywhere this time of the year. Some were skittering along by themselves or just trying to turn right-side up.

But she had no time for this! She had a ton of questions to ask the wolf. Shaking her head as if to scold herself from getting distracted by dung beetles, she broke into a run.

Huffing and puffing from sprinting, she finally reached her most comfortable spot next to the big oak tree.

A squeaking noise from above caught her attention. A raccoon peered out from a hole and looked down at her. It must have been the mother who took care of the cute little babies Lily saw each spring.

"Hello Mama Raccoon, how are you today?" Lily asked.

"Fine, thanks, and how was your first day at school?" the raccoon replied.

"You can talk, too?"

"Yes, of course." The raccoon looked proud.

"How did you know about my new school?"

"Every animal in this forest knows, Lily."

A sudden rustle of leaves interrupted their conversation.

Lily looked up and saw a large animal in the far distance and held her breath. As the animal gingerly walked toward her, she saw that it was Alo.

He stopped right in front of her and sat down.

"Yes, Lily, you can communicate with animals, all animals. You were granted that gift the day you were born. We spoke to you, and you listened, but you were not ready to understand and communicate with us. Until now."

His voice calmed her down. Not only because he really did sound like her dad. It was as if he was singing a lullaby when he spoke. Soft, but deep and melodious.

"Ready to understand and communicate? What do you mean?" Lily asked.

"Let's take a walk."

Lily looked up to say goodbye to the mama raccoon, but she had already disappeared back into the hole in the tree.

Lily and Alo sauntered toward the small river that ran through the forest. They stopped at the edge and sat down. This was where Lily had watched tadpoles swimming frantically in circles and dragonflies soaring gracefully over the water.

"You were always able to listen to animals, but you were not able to concentrate on our messages. You were too young to understand. Now, you are at the right age to explore where your heart leads your journey. One that will take you on many adventures."

"Wow, really? Where am I going?"

"It all lies within your heart, Lily. Your heart will decide what adventures you will go on. Listen," Alo perked up his ears, "to the sounds of the forest. What do you hear?"

"Birds chirping!" Lily smiled.

"Sit down, close your eyes, and listen again."

Lily sat down again, took a deep breath, and closed her eyes.

After a few minutes, she saw a faint image in her mind. She couldn't make it out. With each second, it got clearer and clearer. "Ack!" Lily jumped as she saw a vision of her younger self sitting in the exact same spot.

Young Lily looked up and smiled at Lily and turned back to watching the tadpoles and dragonflies without a care in the world. It was springtime.

"Kerplunk!" A sudden noise caught her attention. It sounded like a small rock hitting the water. Her younger self must have heard it too because she got up and headed toward the sound. Walking into the shallow river, young Lily picked up a shiny object lying on the river bottom.

What is it? Lily moved closer but couldn't see it clearly enough. She only saw young Lily put it in her pocket and walk out of the river.

The vision suddenly vanished into thin air.

"What did she, err, I, put in my pocket?" Lily walked back to Alo.

"It was a coin, a powerful object — a guide of sorts. The person holding the coin can activate all the magical and dark secrets, inspiration, and mystery of this beautiful forest. You, Lily, are that person."

"I remember that coin. I put it in my jewelry box but haven't thought about it since that day." Lily sat down in amazement.

"Well, it is time you think about it again. With this coin, you can see the darkness that lies in this forest, and in this world.

You will also see how to recover its light. I will teach you how to read it, but it will be up to you to follow its lead."

"How to read it? What are you talking about? You can't read a coin."

"Of course you can. That coin has much to say."

"Hhmm, okay, whatever you say. At this point, I'll believe anything." She turned to Alo. "Last night, you said something about healing her." Lily remembered what she wanted to ask Alo earlier. "What exactly did you mean by that?"

"Thousands of years ago, Earth was in balance. Our Mother prospered, along with every plant and animal. She was able to take care of us because nature and humans lived in perfect harmony. Humans hunted as naturally and instinctually as a wolf family. They only took what they needed at that time, and each individual being had a specific task so that they could only survive together.

"But after time passed, humans became plentiful and began to believe they were superior to nature. They started to hunt for fun and called it a sport. They captured animals and put them in small cages to be kept inside their homes or taken to buildings to be studied, stared at, and abused. They tore apart families; separating newborn babies from their mothers. But this suffering was not just with animals. Plants, forests, deserts, oceans, and polar regions are also in danger. That is our reality today. That is our planet Earth as we now know it."

Tears started to form. Lily looked down to see her hands shaking. "I know, some people can be very cruel to animals. And our environment."

"Mother takes care of us. She flies high to watch over and protect us all." Alo's head sunk. "But, she cannot fly high anymore as she is ill. Every time a human hand harms an animal, she loses a feather from her wing. When an animal is saved, a new feather grows in its place. There used to be a balance, but now, more animals are being harmed than saved, and she is losing feathers faster than she can grow them back.

"Soon, she will no longer be able to fly and protect us. The plant and animal world as we know it will be destroyed without our sacred Mother. We will all die, humans as well. Without her, there will be no water to drink, no air to breathe, and no life to live.

"Mother is in much pain and needs our help. She needs your help, Lily. You understand us and have the power and compassion to help us."

"Me? I'm just a young girl. How am I supposed to have the power to save your mother? Where is she anyway? How can a wolf have wings? This is very confusing!"

5

MOTHER NATURE IS REAL

"She is the Mother of all living organisms, so she did not give birth to me," Alo chuckled. "She is the one who protects us all, you too. She is Mother Nature."

"What? Mother Nature really exists?" Lily looked up in hopes she would see her flying above.

"Yes, of course, she is real."

"I don't know how to save anyone though, especially Mother Nature. I'm only ten," Lily lowered her head.

"And I am only five. What is your point?" Alo rolled his eyes.

She looked up at him and smiled. "But how can I help her?"

"That is what we need to figure out together. First of all, are you willing to help her?" Alo asked with big puppy dog eyes.

Lily shrugged her shoulders. "I guess I can try. The last thing I want is for her to die. That would be horrible."

"The coin will show you the right path to bring harmony back between humans and nature," Alo said. "But, the coin only communicates with you when you give it your most precious resource ... your time."

"What do you mean with 'bring back harmony'?" Lily cocked her head.

"When humans respect Mother Nature and all she takes care of, they are at peace with themselves. When they are at peace with themselves, they are at peace with others. And when balance and harmony resides in every human soul, there is world peace.

"When you follow the coin's path, many animals will be saved, and Mother Nature will be healed. Saving animals is only the beginning to bring peace, harmony, and balance to our world, and it will take a lot of time and work, as well as compassion, which comes naturally to you. I have faith in you, Lily. We all do.

"Know that you are not alone. I am here to answer any of your questions and to guide you. You have many friends in this forest. They will come when you call. We are all here to help you along the way."

Lily listened, shaking her head the entire time, not believing her own ears.

I can't wait to tell Eva and Till! They will freak out! Or will they? They already think I'm crazy for going into the forest alone. What if they laugh at me and say I'm dreaming or something? Hhmm, maybe I better keep quiet.

Beep! Her phone disrupted her thoughts.

"It is getting late. Go home to your parents. We will meet again very soon." Alo bowed his head and trotted off.

Lily heard a howl from a distance. She lifted her head and howled back. Surprised she was able to make such a powerful sound, she flashed a wide smile up to the sky. The sun was setting.

Breathing in deeply, she closed her eyes and listened carefully. The forest was silent.

The little hairs on her arms stood straight up as a chilly wave flowed over her body.

She shook herself back to warmth, but that didn't help her fear of this new, mysterious challenge.

Save Mother Nature, yeah right! Good joke!

She knew better, though. This was no joke. This was real!

Walking through the small clearing along her path, she heard the caw of a raven. This was not uncommon in enchanted Reinhardswald, but the sound was closer than she was accustomed. The raven was only a few meters above her head, circling around her. It cawed a few more times, and Lily listened. And understood. "Call me, call me ... Call me, call me."

The raven then swooped down and flew right past Lily's head, making her duck. The second time the raven swooped, she whispered, "Call me when you need help. Call me."

Before leaving the clearing, Lily cawed back just to see if she could imitate this sound. She could.

Lily cuddled with her mom on the couch before going upstairs to get ready for bed. "Mom, have you ever had to help someone who was in danger?"

"What kind of danger? Lily, what's wrong?"

"Oh, no, it's not like that. I was just wondering." Lily paused to think of something to say. "I watched something on TV the other night about social workers who help teens on the street, and it can get pretty dangerous out there," Lily said, feeling proud of her quick answer.

"That's true. Social workers have a very important and fulfilling job. I can't say I could do that myself, but I really admire those who can. But to answer your question, yes, I have helped a few people in danger. Not in a life or death situation but with other serious issues that are a bit too complex to discuss now."

"How did you know you did the right thing, Mom?"

"Because I saw how happy they were after I helped them. And I know if I was ever in danger, they would want to help me, too. I also know that you and Daddy would be the first people by my side. I actually think you'd make a great social worker."

Feeling a rush of energy stream over her whole body, Lily smiled and hugged her mom even tighter. Lily's mom always made her feel good about herself, probably without even knowing it.

Lily held on tight to her mom and hummed to the music playing in the background. Her dad was listening to his favorite rock station. Lily preferred pop and the charts, but when she heard her dad's music, it made her feel comfortable and at home.

Her dad sang and hummed while reading the newspaper. *How could he read the paper and sing at the same time?* She loved listening to him sing, sometimes more than the music itself.

"Okay, Pumpkin, time for bed," Lily's dad said.

"Oh, alright. It's still early though," Lily pleaded.

"It's 8:00, time for bed."

Lily got up from the warm, cuddly spot next to her mom and went upstairs to get ready for bed.

After dilly-dallying for about twenty minutes, she called downstairs to her parents, "I'm in bed now, tuck me in."

"Thanks, Mom," Lily said as soon as they walked in her room.

"For what?"

"For being you. And you too, Dad. You rock!"

"No, YOU rock!"

"We could do this all night, Dad," Lily chuckled.

"We love you too, dear," her mom said, giving Lily a kiss on her forehead.

After they left, Lily laid in bed, thinking about her new challenge.

And then she remembered. The coin! She sprang up, turned on the light and looked in her jewelry box. There it was, still shiny, just lying amongst her earrings. It was the size of a two-euro coin; gold with a silver inlay on one side.

On the solid gold side, she saw a fern imprint with writing over it: "Nature heals." On the silver inlay, there was an illustration of what resembled an angel standing in a forest with these words on top: "Protect our Mother."

That must be Mother Nature. Wow, she's beautiful. Lily tucked the coin in a small, purple velvet jewelry bag and hid it safely in the top drawer of her nightstand.

As she crawled back underneath the covers, her phone beeped. It was Eva.

"Hey, whatcha doing? My mom's working the night shift, so I'm here all alone again. Not that I'm scared or anything. It's just, well, a bit eerie and I'm having a hard time falling asleep."

"Wanna sleep over here?"

"No, I'm in bed already. Just wanted to chat with you. Thought it would help me fall asleep."

Not five minutes later, Eva texted Lily again. "Did you hear that? It sounded like a wolf. It sounded like it was right in my backyard! I'm kinda scared now, can I come over?"

"Sure, I'll ask my mom if she can pick you up. Get your stuff ready."

Lily also heard the wolf's cry but smiled, knowing who it was.

She went downstairs to ask her mom, who was sitting in her rocker reading a book.

"Oh, poor Eva. Okay, I'll text her mom and pick her up in a jiffy."

Lily was waiting with the door open when her mom pulled into the driveway.

"Thank you," Eva said as she carried her overnight bag toward the house.

"Eva, you know you're always welcome at our house and that your mom is doing the best she can, right? I wish I could help more," Lily's mom said.

"You help us out a lot. I wish I could stay at home when Mom has to work the night shift. She's already depressed about getting a divorce, so I don't want her to feel worse or guilty. But when I try to go to sleep, I get so scared sometimes. Did you hear that wolf cry? It was so loud that I could even hear it with the window closed."

"I heard something but didn't really know what it was. There are wolves in this area, and sometimes, when the wind is right, I can hear more than one. I find them fascinating and am glad they're back again," Lily's mom said.

"Me, too!" Lily said, thinking of Alo.

"Yeah, I'm glad they're coming back too, but I would never want to meet one face to face," Eva replied.

"Well, there's no bad wolf here," Lily answered.

"Good night, Lily. Good night, Eva." her mom said, ushering the girls upstairs.

"You're the best friend anyone could have," Eva whispered to Lily as they walked upstairs.

"You're the best, too, Eva."

After a few minutes of talking about their first day of school, the girls settled down and fell asleep.

6
———

SCHOOL BLUES

Lily and Eva got ready for school the next morning and met Till
at the bus stop. They were quiet and yawning during most of
the bus trip while Till rambled on about soccer practice the
other day.

"What? I'm serious, I kicked backwards - in midair - and
made a goal!" Till said, responding to Lily's head shaking.

"Oh, I believe you, Till, sorry. I was just thinking about
something else."

Still tired, Lily stood up when they reached the school. On
the way out of the bus, she tripped on the steps and rammed
into the girl in front of her. They both landed hard on the
ground next to each other.

As they got up and started to rub themselves off, Lily apologized profusely. Then they looked at each other. It was Viktoria.
"Oh, of course, it's you again. Your clumsy self had better keep
away from me or else," Viktoria scoffed and sauntered away.

Lily turned around and saw Till trying to rush out of the
bus. Maybe he saw her fall.

How embarrassing.

"Are you okay?" Marc asked as he ran toward Lily with a horrified look on his face.

"Yeah. I'm so clumsy. I can't believe I've already done this twice now!"

"Geez, Lily, what was that all about?" Till appeared by her side. "I saw you and Viktoria getting up from the ground. What happened?"

"Oh, it was nothing, but I better be super careful from now on," Lily said.

"If you run into any trouble with her, just let me know, okay?" Till said. "I gotta run. See you later."

"There she is, Ms. Pusher and Shover. Let's see if she dares to push me just one more time," Viktoria said to her friends as they walked past.

Lily looked at Marc, clenching her teeth.

"Come on, let's go to our classroom." He wrapped his arm around Lily and guided her down the hall.

Concentrating on schoolwork was especially difficult that day. Lily's busy mind raced with thoughts of Viktoria, her own clumsiness, sympathy for Eva, and her new gift of being able to communicate with animals. And of course, her new friend, Alo.

I just want to go home. She wanted to know more about Mother Nature, but it wasn't time yet. She still had lunch and then two more classes.

When their math class ended, Lily and Eva packed up their stuff and headed toward the cafeteria to meet Till. Lily was walking to the table when all of a sudden someone barged into her, causing her to flip over her tray onto the floor. She looked up.

"Better watch where you're going, Missy." Viktoria snickered, turned around, and strutted away, pointy nose in the air.

"Oh, Lily, here, let me help you," Eva said.

Till also dashed to the rescue and quickly took the tray with the wasted food to the cleanup station.

"We have enough food for the three of us, just take what you want," he offered.

"She hates me already, and it's only the second day of school. Ugh, what am I going to do, Till?" Lily cried.

"Lily, you are strong, and we're here to help you, but I would suggest being a little less clumsy. That would certainly help," Till said, raising one eyebrow and topping it off with a smirk.

"Yeah, I guess that would help," Lily admitted.

"We're always here for you," Eva said.

"Thanks, you two are the best!"

"Don't worry too much. She may be mean to you but isn't going to kill you," Till said.

"Well, at least I don't have to worry about what I want on my tombstone just yet," Lily joked with a nervous smile.

On the way back from lunch, Viktoria and her friends walked past Lily but ignored her. *Whew.*

They spent the last hour and a half of the school day in art class, which Lily loved. She was able to draw fairly well; not as well as Eva, but well enough. And on this day, she drew a wolf.

"Very impressive," Lily's art teacher said, looked over her shoulder.

The final bell rang.

Lily and Eva packed their bags and walked to the bus stop.

On the way, Lily noticed a little green grasshopper on the path. She bent down to inspect it more closely.

"Creech, crickety crick, crick."

"Um, Lily, what are you doing? It sounds like you're grinding your teeth or something. What's wrong?" Eva asked.

Realizing that she had just asked the grasshopper if it was okay if she could move him to safety, she brushed it off. "Oh, oh, um, nothing, not important. I was just practicing my cricket sound making. I saw a video the other day of a guy who made all sorts of animal sounds, and I thought it was funny. Want to hear me speak ladybugish?"

"Uh, no- I'm good. Thanks anyway," Eva chuckled. "Hey, I don't think we'll see each other this weekend. I want to spend time with my mom. Tomorrow would have been their wedding anniversary, so I don't want her to be sad about this stupid divorce."

"Oh, I'm sorry. Sure, that's fine. I have no idea what we have planned anyway." Lily hoped her parents didn't plan anything because all she wanted to do was to spend time with her new forest friends.

After getting off the bus, Lily said bye to Eva and sprinted home.

Her parents were both still at work, so Lily was free to do anything.

"I'm sorry, Ralph, I have to go meet Alo again. I'll be back a little later." Lily stopped for a minute to rub his neck, which he adored. Afterward, she grabbed the pouch with the coin in it and ran back downstairs, through the door, and into the woods.

Once Lily arrived at the big oak tree, she closed her eyes, looked up, and howled. "Aaaaaaloooooooooo, where are youuuuuuuu?"

She looked around but only saw an army of tall spruce trees in this part of the Reinhardswald.

Lily loved living here, smack dab in the middle of the Brothers Grimm Fairy Tale Route. Her house was not far from Kassel, near Bergpark Wilhelmshöhe, a UNESCO World Heritage Site, but more interesting, she lived very close to the Dornröschenschloss Sababurg, Sleeping Beauty's Castle, and the surrounding Tierpark, a huge animal preservation area with many amazing animals and also the home of a beautiful wolf family.

I wonder if they know Alo and his family?

Lily suddenly thought of the 'big, bad wolf' in one of her favorite fairy tales, Little Red Riding Hood. Her parents often read the original Brothers Grimm versions in both German and

English, depending on who was reading. Her mom always read in German and her dad in English.

The Brothers Grimm never sugarcoated anything either, which Lily really enjoyed. She liked to know the truth, no matter how gruesome. She didn't like it though when the hunters filled the wolf's belly with stones and left him to die when all he needed was food.

That's so sad. Wolves need to eat too!

She also knew this was an old, traditional story to teach children not to talk to strangers and so really had nothing to do with wolves, but still, portraying wolves like that was mean and inaccurate.

The faint sound of dried leaves crunching caught her attention away from fairy tales. Lily turned around with excitement, only to see it was a bird on the ground looking for worms. When she looked back up though, she saw Alo's head appear in the small clearing ahead. He walked closer and closer, came right up to her face, and sniffed her mouth. "Whoa, I thought you were going to lick me," Lily said.

"This is how we greet other," he said.

"Well, I guess it's better than smelling butts like dogs. Next time though, I'll make sure I brush my teeth," Lily said, covering her mouth. She had eaten spaghetti with garlic and onions for lunch.

"Please do not do that! I love the smell of Italian food! How was school today?"

"Okay, I guess. I made a few mistakes, and will have to pay for them," Lily replied, thinking of Viktoria.

"There is only one way to handle bullies. Do you know what that is?" Alo asked.

"How did you know I was talking about a bully in school? You can't read my thoughts now, can you?" Lily asked.

"Yes, I can. When the moon is full, I can read your thoughts."

"I'll have to remember that! So, what do you think I should do?" Lily asked curiously.

"Put me on a leash and bring me to show and tell." Alo bared his teeth and growled ferociously. Foamy slobber formed on the corners of his mouth.

Startled, Lily stepped back and stiffened. Thoughts of her recent nightmare flashed in her head. Her body was warming up from fear.

Alo immediately stopped and sat down. "I apologize, I did not mean to scare you!"

Relieved, Lily drew in a deep breath. "I wish I could take you to school!"

Lily took the coin out of her bag. "You told me you would teach me how to read this coin."

Alo looked at it lying in her palm. "Ah, yes, I see it has not changed yet."

"When will it change?" Lily asked.

"When you concentrate on the coin, it awakens. And if Mother Nature needs your help, it will change to show you a path to take."

7

BREAK THE CHAINS

Alo closed his eyes, pointed his nose to the sky, and let out a loud, deep howl. The birds immediately stopped chirping. The trees stopped shaking their leaves. Dead silence then filled the air. Alo howled again.

The wind began to whirl around them, starting at Lily's feet, then moving up her body, pulling her long thick brown hair straight up over her head, as if every strand was waving at the sky. The trees rattled their branches again, shaking off the dead autumn leaves, fluttering them into circles above the trees.

A bright spotlight shone on Lily, forcing her to put her hands over her eyes. The heat from the light warmed her hands and face. Curiously, she peeked through her fingers but couldn't see anything but the blinding white light.

"Ouch," she dropped the coin. "It burnt my hand!" She looked down at the shining red fluorescent coin.

"Do not touch it." Alo ran over to the river, took a few slurps, came back, and spat on the coin. Sssssst. The water bubbled until it evaporated into thin air. The coin turned back to its normal color.

Lily picked it up gently and looked at it. It no longer showed the fern. Instead, there was an illustration of a chain with the message "Break all chains." On the silver inlay, there was a small skeleton inside a cage. On the bottom, it read "Beauty has no boundaries."

She showed the coin to Alo who slowly sat down, closed his eyes, and lowered his head. She wanted to ask him what was wrong, but her instincts stopped her because he looked so peaceful and she didn't want to disturb him.

"Lily," Alo finally said. "What do you know about the human face?"

"Well, I'll probably get pimples soon," Lily said. "My mom complains that stress irritates the skin on her face, but I don't really understand that. Oh, and I know that when I get older, I'll get wrinkles. My grandma told me to be proud of every one of them when I get to be her age because wrinkles mean that you're wise. I also know that there are several layers of skin on my face and that the sun is dangerous, so I have to smear sunblock all over my body."

She paused. "Why are you asking?"

"Do you know that humans make products to help themselves look young and beautiful?" Alo asked.

"My mom smears cream on her face twice a day, but I don't think it makes her look any more beautiful or younger. She still looks the same to me. She also uses makeup when she goes out at night."

"Do you know how those products are made?" Alo asked.

"Are you talking about cosmetics? Yes, I know what they are, but I don't know how they're made."

"They are made with many different kinds of ingredients," Alo said. "Some are good for your skin, but others are not. Before a product is sold to a human, it has to be tested. Some products are tested on animals to see if they have a reaction."

"A reaction? What does that mean?" Lily asked.

"A reaction is a side effect. If you use a moisturizing cream on your face and develop a rash after a few days, or you get a few pimples, something in that cream made your skin react negatively to it. You would not be able to use that product anymore unless you like rashes and zits," Alo scoffed.

Lily shook her head.

"Companies that sell these products are required to make sure they are safe and do not cause harmful side effects. Since humans are so different, what works on one person may not work on the other, so they have to perform many tests. Some companies test their products on animals and cause a lot of harm to those animals."

"That doesn't seem fair. Have they ever tested on you?" Lily asked.

"No, I am too strong and dangerous. They test on weaker, innocent animals. They are called lab animals and were either taken from the wild or the streets, then put in small cages to live for the rest of their lives. Many are even born in cages because it is cheaper for humans to breed them than to spend time catching them. Lab experiments are usually performed on rats, mice, rabbits, monkeys, cats, and dogs."

"Cats and dogs, too?" Lily's big brown eyes popped out like a cartoon figure.

"Every day, these animals are harmed in unnatural ways, brought back to their cages half-dead to rest up for the next day of torture. Several companies do not test on animals, but many still do. And companies do not just test on animals in the cosmetic industry but also in the medical field. The ingredients in most, if not all, medicines have been tested on animals."

"The coin showed you a message from Mother Nature," Alo continued. "She is asking for your help."

"Does she want me to help lab animals? How?" Lily asked.

"The coin will show you how. Go home now and watch it carefully. Meet me here tomorrow." Alo turned and walked away.

Lily drug her feet on the walk home. Tears formed in her eyes. She never felt this kind of sorrow before. Not even when her grandma passed away because that seemed natural. Her grandma was old, and as her mom said at the funeral, "It was her time to go." But this felt different. This didn't feel natural or normal at all. It felt traumatic and overwhelming because she had also never been asked to save anything. She wasn't a super-hero. She was just a young girl who didn't really know how to save anyone.

Numbness overcame her. Unable to continue walking, she sank to the ground and wept.

Head hung low; she spotted a few ants on the ground.

More and more ants arrived and started to form a circle around Lily. Hundreds of them marched in unison, as if they'd rehearsed this moment every day over the past few weeks.

Lily leaned forward and asked what they were doing.

One ant walked up to her and stood on his hind legs. "We want to thank you for helping us."

"But I don't even know how to help you. I'm just a little girl."

"And we are even littler, but look at what we can do? Each of us can move objects that are fifty times heavier than our own weight. And look at what we can move together? Logs of wood! It is amazing, is it not? So, no, you are not little, Lily. You are the right size to be able to move mountains."

"Huh, I never thought about it like that before. Thanks so much, I feel a lot better now, and you're welcome for helping you. I'll definitely try my very best! I have to go home now, but before I go, I have just one more question: How can I avoid stepping on you? You're everywhere, and I can't always see you down there."

"Oh, do not worry about that. When we do not have enough time to get out of the way, we get in between the leaves so that we do not have a full-impact squishy situation. It usually works, but sometimes, an ant does get killed.

"But it is not your fault," the ant continued. "That is nature, and we understand that humans cannot walk on air. No matter how sad it is to lose a friend, we do not blame you for the death of an ant or any other insect!"

"That's good to hear, thank you. And you're pretty clever, that's for sure. Well, I gotta go now and thanks again, I really appreciate it."

She beat her parents home, so just went upstairs to her room to rest.

She held onto the coin so tightly that when she sat on her bed and opened her hand, she could see the chain imprint on her palm. Squinting to inspect her hand more closely, she noticed something had moved in the image. A piece of the chain broke off! She looked back at the coin to find the same broken chain.

Huh, interesting.

Lily stared at the coin, turning it over many times, for what seemed to be an hour. Thoughts of caged-up lab animals filled her mind when she heard her mom walk in the door.

"Lily, are you home?"

"Yeah, Mom, I'm upstairs."

"Okay, I'll start cooking dinner, your dad will be home any minute."

Lily laid in bed with the coin lying on her chest and rested her eyes. The thoughts didn't disappear though.

"Dinner's ready! Come on down, Lily," her mom interrupted her thoughts. "We're having pizza!" Relieved to hear something positive, Lily rushed downstairs.

After dinner, Lily took out a board game from the cabinet and set it up.

Every Friday night after dinner, unless they had another engagement, the Bowers family played board games, something Lily usually couldn't wait to do. Tonight was different though.

"I want to do some research for school tonight, so can we only play this one game?"

"Homework on a Friday night, is that necessary?" Lily's dad asked.

"It's not necessary, but I'm really interested in the subject and can't stop thinking about it. Please?"

"By all means, learn away, Hun," her dad said. "What's the subject?"

"Animal testing," Lily answered.

"Animal testing, that's a pretty in-depth subject. I'm surprised you're covering this during your first week in school," he said.

"It was mentioned in biology, and I just want to learn more, that's all." Lily hoped no more questions would come.

After one round of a mystery 'Whodunit' board game, Lily went upstairs and checked the coin for any changes. But nothing happened.

She turned on the laptop she got as a birthday present last February and searched for articles related to animal testing.

8

FEATHERLESS WINGS

After reading and watching a few videos, she stopped, put her head in her hands, and cried again.

So much torture, who does this? Universities, research facilities, and companies that make household products, medicines, cosmetics, food, pesticides, industrial chemicals...

Realizing that she and everyone else on this planet bought stuff that had been tested on, she cried even more.

After calming down, Lily continued her research and found out that animals were forced to eat or inhale substances; either that or some cream was rubbed on a shaved part of their head or a fluid injected into their skin. Sometimes those substances were toxic, too.

How horrible.

She then watched a video of monkeys waking up with huge cylinder tubes coming out of the top of their heads after brain surgery. While their heads bled, they were forced to perform mundane tasks and were deprived of water. All this to learn how their brain and vision worked.

Lily's stomach rolled over a few times.

Running to the bathroom, Lily closed the door and opened the toilet seat cover. But nothing came out.

She sat there for a moment, gagging and breathing heavily. A bead of sweat slid down her forehead.

She finally got up slowly, rinsed her face with cold water, put her hair in a ponytail, and looked at herself in the mirror.

I have to stop this torture! This is unacceptable!

Feeling exhausted, she got dressed in her pajamas, brushed her teeth, and crawled into bed. Pictures of bloody, screaming monkeys and frightened, shaved and cut up rabbits invaded her mind.

There was no way she could sleep. Not even being read to by her mom would help at this point.

She drudgingly got up and logged back onto her computer.

Whew! She found out that animal testing was banned in the European Union in 2013.

But further research showed that this ban was only on the final product, not on each individual ingredient or element in a product.

So, while there were a few laws that protected animals, there were loopholes which allowed companies to continue to test on animals.

Well, that's sneaky and downright wrong!

She researched more and found more laws and more loopholes.

What shocked her most was when she found out that many tests done on animals were useless on humans, making them inaccurate and risky.

Why? Lily turned off her computer and laid on her bed, in complete silence.

I can't stop this. There's nothing I can do. They've been torturing animals for decades and won't stop because some ten-year-old girl asked them to. People won't change. Even large animal rights organizations can't stop them. They've won a few battles, but not the war.

Feeling overwhelmed and sadder than she'd ever felt in her entire life, she got up and opened her balcony door. The whistling wind and cool breeze felt really good on her teary, hot face.

The trees were waving back and forth. Not thinking clearly, she waved back.

Oh, that was silly.

But then, one tree bent his crown forward and swayed to the right and left a few times.

Okay, so now the trees are talking to me? This is insane!

Not wanting to appear rude, Lily waved again, closed the door, and crawled under the covers, and eventually she fell asleep.

Startled by a blinding light, Lily sat straight up in bed. Carefully opening her eyes, she went to the window and looked out.

Squinting, Lily couldn't see anything except bright white light. The entire backyard was lit up. She opened the balcony door and stepped out. As soon as the light started to fade, she was able to see more clearly.

A glowing figure resembling a woman glided up to Lily's balcony. Gasping, Lily stepped back and stood motionless in the doorway.

The figure had a woman's face, arms, and hands. Her big round green eyes were that of a cat. The rest of her body was a colorful collage of fur, feathers, scales, leaves, mushrooms, branches, and flowers flowing from her head all the way down to the ground outside like the train of a wedding dress.

Is that a waterfall?

Lily's eyes must have been popping out of her head when she noticed that her hair was part normal hair and part water. Even fish were swimming in it!

As the figure reached the balcony, Lily moved back into her room and invited her inside. She had no doubt who was visiting her.

Lily sat on her bed and waited in silence to hear what this beautiful vision had to say.

Instead of talking, she opened her wings as wide as they would stretch. Lily gasped in horror upon noticing her wings, which were severely ruffled and almost featherless!

Alo wasn't kidding. Lily remembered him saying that Mother Nature could barely fly because she had lost too many feathers.

"They usually grow back completely, but now, as soon as a feather comes in, it falls out immediately. If I lose all my feathers, I will no longer be able to protect the beautiful plants and animals on Earth. I will die without a purpose and if I die, so will every living organism on this planet," Mother Nature said. "Lily, you are my only hope."

"I'm just a kid though. I'd love to save you, I really would, but I don't know how." Lily lowered her head.

"You are very young, yes, but you have something no one else has, Lily: the talent to communicate with me and all I look after. You are also intelligent and courageous and have the most powerful gift of all - compassion! With your ambition and love, you will be able to save us all. I cannot see the future, but my instincts have never failed me in the past. You, Lily, are our savior."

Say what? I'm no savior! And how can I be talking to Mother Nature, this is insane! I must be dreaming!

Lily picked up Ralph to see if he was still able to talk, to see if all of this was real, but he was dead asleep in his shell. She carefully put him back, remembering that turtles didn't like to be picked up.

Mother Nature glided over to Lily's desk and picked up the coin. "This coin will guide you. I see that the chain broke. Do you know what that means?"

"No, but I think it has something to do with helping lab animals. Lab animals wear chains. Am I supposed to break their chains and free them?"

"If only it were that easy," Mother Nature answered. "That is your ultimate goal: to save animals and help me bring back the balance between nature and the human world. But this is just the beginning; there are many problems we face. I am not willing to continue enabling natural disasters that disrupt and ruin more lives. It breaks my heart. The obvious signs are apparently not working, so I now feel we need the help of a powerful human being, and that human being is you! Can you help us?"

"More than ever!" Lily exclaimed. "Um, actually, I still have no clue what to do," she added, realizing she answered too quickly.

"Thank you, Lily. Watch this coin closely. It will show you every step of the way. The broken chain is a symbol of freedom, the ultimate goal. How you achieve that goal will be shown in the coin, so watch it closely."

"When will it change again?" Lily asked.

"When the time is right. It is getting late. I better leave you alone now. Tomorrow, come into the woods, to the big oak tree, and bring the coin. I will meet you there. Sleep well, and thank you again, Lily; your heart is bigger than life." Mother Nature vanished quickly and left white sparkles in her place.

Lily sat and stared at the wall. She felt a surge of energy move from her left foot all the way up to her head. Shivering, she quickly crawled under the covers.

"Did you see her, Ralph?" Lily asked, but Ralph didn't respond again.

Figures, he wakes up when I sneeze in the middle of the night but misses a visit from Mother Nature. Typical tortoise.

Lily turned on the light to look at the coin. It started to change as soon as she picked it up. *Don't blink now!*

The chain transformed into a ring of six hands holding each other in a circle. She turned it over and saw a heart with the words "With a little help from your friends" in the middle.

Lily started thinking about Eva and Till, her closest friends. Together, they had six hands!

Of course, that's it! There's no way I can do all this by myself. I need help too!

Lily knew they would do anything for her because she would do anything for them. *I have the best friends in the world!*

She thought again of how insane this was and what they would think and then remembered that she thought it best not to tell them.

But this is a sign. Maybe I should tell them? Sigh. No need to worry about this now though.

She was exhausted and wanted to crawl into bed.

Not a minute after she laid her head on her pillow, she was dreaming of her Reinhardswald, but this time, it looked like a tub of rainbow paint was poured over it.

The beech tree trunks were sky blue and had royal blue leaves, the ferns were bright pink, and the deer were a beautiful deep purple with flashy golden eyes.

She was cheerfully jumping and skipping through the narrow path until she came to a dead end. Looking around, she saw that the path behind her had disappeared. There was no way to go but forward.

The beech tree in front of her leaned forward with one of its branches inviting her to walk up. She walked all the way up to the top and could see the entire forest just like an eagle flying above.

But it wasn't a pretty sight. It was devastating. Everything around her was black and gray and full of soot and ash, as if everything had completely burnt down. The trees remained standing but were bare and dry. The entire forest looked dead.

She climbed back down the tree and looked up from the

bottom. Everything was colorful again, just like when she started walking up the tree. The path behind her also reappeared.

She saw Mother Nature in a small clearing sitting with her legs crossed, head in her hands, sobbing silently.

Lily approached her and said, "Are you okay?"

As Mother Nature looked up, a cold wind blew over Lily's body. There were black holes where Mother Nature's cat's eyes used to be.

"Aaaaa!" Lily screamed and woke up shivering in a cold sweat.

She breathed in deeply with relief that it was just a dream.

The warm, sweet smell of fresh maple syrup filled her nostrils. Pancakes. Lily's favorite meal.

At least there was something to look forward to.

9

MANY NEW FRIENDS

Lily's feet — and heavy heart — drug as she walked downstairs.

Her mom was flipping pancakes in the skillet. "Hey, want to go to the park today, sweetie? The weather's beautiful, and we thought we could have a picnic and play frisbee or go on a bike tour or something. What do you think?"

"I have some homework to do, and I'd like to spend the rest of the afternoon with Eva if that's okay. She really needs a friend right now."

"Oh, I understand. I'd want to do the same thing. You're a good friend! Eva's mom has been working too hard lately, even on the weekends. Maybe it's time I have a heart-to-heart with her."

"Glad that's settled," Lily's dad said impatiently. "Let's eat some breakfast. I'm starving!" He turned into a growling bear when he was hungry. "Actually, it would be good to get some garden work done. I didn't mow the lawn last week, and now it looks like a jungle out there!"

Whew. She doesn't like to lie, but today, she had no choice. An important but very scary job awaited her!

"Mom, do you buy cruelty-free cosmetics and household cleaning products?" Lily asked.

"Yes, or I try to anyway. It can be difficult though because, with some products, there are no alternatives or information about testing," Lily's mom said.

After breakfast, Lily went upstairs into her bathroom and opened the cabinet. She noticed the cruelty-free symbol on a few products but not on all of them.

She also knew from her research last night that not every animal-test-free product had that symbol on the packaging. Sometimes the companies didn't go through the process to receive the official cruelty-free certification, even though it didn't seem that difficult or expensive. In fact, it was free to get certified, but the company would have to pay a fee to print the symbol on the packaging.

And what does, "We're against animal testing," mean? Do they test or not? Ugh, why is this SO difficult?

Lily made three piles. One for those products that didn't test, one for those that had nothing on the label, and one for those that said they were against animal testing but there was no actual proof of it.

"What are you doing?" Her mom walked in, seeing Lily surrounded by products scattered all over the floor.

"Checking to see if they're cruelty-free," Lily said.

"Oh, let me help you with that."

Her mom sat down on the floor with her and looked over every product with her. She took the products that either didn't have a label or needed further research downstairs to check herself.

"I'll let you know about these, and I promise you, if I find out they test on animals, I will no longer buy them, okay?"

"Thanks, Mom, we really appreciate it."

"We?" Lily's mom asked.

"Yeah, the animals and I."

"You're so sweet," her mom said and went downstairs.

Lily made a list of the brand names left on the floor that were cruelty-free and then put them back into the cabinet.

Feeling relieved that most of the products they had were cruelty-free, she went into her room and took out her homework.

To concentrate on multiplication now though was useless. All she could think of was how she would be able to help Mother Nature.

She had no clue, and the coin, even though it gave her clues, wasn't much help at all.

She gave up on math and decided to wake up early on Sunday to get it done before breakfast. She asked her dad if she could finish her homework in the morning and visit Eva now.

"No problem. Have a nice time, and be home by seven at the latest," he said.

Lily walked in the direction to Eva's house. After turning the corner, she went into the woods so that her dad wouldn't see her.

Nervous and a bit scared, Lily's feet couldn't walk her fast enough. Reinhardswald was even more magical and mysterious than she could ever imagine.

She believed in parts of the fairy tales that were told by the Brothers Grimm. Of course, not everything, but that's what made their stories so interesting. If they only spoke the truth, there'd be no magic.

Or ... maybe there would be? Maybe they DID experience the same kind of magic?

Suddenly, her knees bent and collapsed to the ground. Frozen, she couldn't move, as her knees were getting dirty from digging into the ground. Numb and weak, she managed to look up slowly and saw Alo a foot away, staring at her.

"It is overwhelming, I know, but you are strong, and with

our help, you can do this, Lily." Alo laid down right beside her and put his head on her leg.

"Alo, I have no clue what to do, and I'm really scared."

"I understand. Just trust your instincts. And Mother Nature."

Startled by the rustling of leaves behind her, Lily turned around to see Mother Nature descending from the sky. She was as beautiful as Lily remembered her, but this time, she was bigger. Much bigger.

"Oh, wow. How did you get so ..." Lily could not get any more words out.

"Outside, in the forest, I am as tall as the trees. Inside, I am as big as any room will allow."

"Did you bring the coin?" Mother Nature asked.

"Uh, yeah, here it is." Lily handed it to her.

After inspecting the coin carefully, Mother Nature looked up and breathed in heavily. Upon breathing out, she slowly turned around and around in circles. A faint wind whistled through the forest. The leaves fluttered while the trees swayed in unison.

Lily could understand the birds' chatter. "What is happening, Mama?" a baby finch chirped in the nearby nest.

"We are being called upon. Stay here, I will be right back." Mama Finch flew down closer to Mother Nature, who whispered something in her little ear. Mama Finch flew back to her nest and cuddled with her babies.

The forest air now smelled like a fresh, crisp fall morning after a long evening rain.

"You are getting help," Mother Nature said.

"I don't think I can tell my friends about you though," Lily said.

"You may be right, Lily. They may not understand."

"But how can I get help if I can't ask my friends? I need them!"

"Your friends are all around, Lily. Open your eyes. They are here. You just have not met them yet."

A larger bird flew to a branch right next to Lily's head and looked at her intently.

"My name is Rae," said the black raven. Rae spread her wings out wide, tucked in her right wing and bowed. "Nice to meet you, Lily."

"Nice to officially meet you as well. I think we've met before." Lily recognized Rae as the raven who cawed at her the other day because the end of her left wing was chopped off. "What happened to your wing?"

"I was hurt a long time ago," Rae said. "I can still fly but need a little more energy to do so. My vision is stronger than my flying capabilities though. I see things others do not."

"And I will help you too," squeaked a tiny mouse who suddenly was on top of Lily's foot. "My name is Serena. I am as quick as a firecracker and can fit in any small space."

Within a minute, Lily was surrounded by many forest animals who came out of the shadows to greet her.

Squirrels, birds, deer, mice, rats, wild boar, foxes, wolves, snakes, and at least a million insects, bees, flies, beetles, and spiders were all staring at her with bright eyes and bushy tails. That is, if they had tails at all.

Tons of animals big and small, weak and strong, stood tall and proud.

Lily looked down at her uncontrollably shaking hands. Extreme heat rose from her belly up to her head. She was sure she was as red as a beet.

Alo walked up to her. Lily bent down and hugged him tightly. She'd never been surrounded by this many wild animals before.

Alo sensed her fear and whispered in her ear, "Do not be scared. They all love and respect you and would never harm you in any way."

Lily's fear slowly faded, and she relaxed her grip.

"There you go, feel the warmth and love. They are waiting for you to speak," Alo said.

Lily stood up tall, looked directly into their eyes, and announced, "It's nice to meet all of you. Your friends are being harmed. I'm so sorry for the pain you all suffer. I can't change the past, but I can try to change the future. But I can only do this with your help. Together, we will save your friends and Mother Nature."

The animals howled, swooned, squeaked, grunted, and cheered as loudly as they could.

Once they turned quiet, Lily continued in a meek voice. "The truth is that I don't know what to do. I don't know how I can help you and Mother Nature. I need your help. Who can help me figure this out?"

Seven animals stepped forward: An owl, a deer, a cat, a fox, a wolf, Serena the mouse, and Rae the raven.

"Wow, so many volunteers, thank you, thank you. I guess we should begin now, what do you think?"

Jumping up, the fox said, "Clever idea!"

Lily turned to the other animals who were watching her intently. "Thank you all for coming, we'll meet again soon."

They bowed and slowly dispersed into the deep, thick woods.

Lily turned back to her group and smiled. "Who do we have here?"

The sleek black cat pranced up to introduce herself. Her name was Moon.

The deer stepped closer to greet Lily. "Hi, I am Trixi and am so glad to finally meet you, Lily. I have been waiting for this moment since I was a young fawn, which was not too long ago. I am only two years old. My mommy told me you are a very special girl and that if I ever met you to tell you that you are loved. So, here goes: Lily, you are loved."

"Oh, you're sweet, thank you, Trixi, it's very nice to meet you. And you too, Moon. Your coat is very sleek and beautiful, by the way."

"I am Alpina," a beautiful silver wolf interrupted. Lily bent down and smiled wide, so Alpina could smell her teeth. "I am the alpha female in Alo's family."

Prancing right up to Lily, the fox said, "Hey, I am Jake, by the way!"

"Nice to meet you, too, Jake!"

Lily then looked at the owl and lifted her left eyebrow.

"Just call me Sam," the owl answered. "My given name is too difficult for humans to speak."

"Thank you, Sam, but now you've made me curious about your name. Can I please hear it?" Lily pleaded.

Sam winked at Lily and projected a noise that was so high pitched, Lily had to cover her ears.

"I'm sorry," Lily said. "It's a beautiful name, but you're right, way too difficult for me."

"Me, too. Please do not ask him to ever do that again, OK?" Moon, the cat, hissed.

"I'm excited you're all here, and thanks for volunteering," Lily said. She started to talk but stopped in mid-sentence. "Wait a minute, how can you all understand me? I'm not barking, howling, growling, clicking, or cooing. What language am I speaking?"

10

BUTTERFLIES

"You are speaking Animalish. It is the universal language that
every animal understands, except humans. Well, every human,
except for you," Sam, the owl, explained.

"You can speak to us individually in our own language,"
Alpina chimed in, "but when you speak to a group of animals
of various species, you automatically speak Animalish. This
came naturally to you and will from now on. Non-human
animals can usually understand other species without too
many communication breakdowns."

"Really? Wow, how cool is that?"

Over the next few hours, they talked about how they could
help lab animals. Her team was well aware of what their friends
had to endure in these labs and already had a few good ideas.

Finally, they came up with a game plan that was not only
clever but realistic. *This may actually work!*

Feeling proud, Lily told them she had to go back home but
would be back in the morning to finish up their work.

As she left the woods, she turned around and spotted a
woodpecker on a tree. He stopped drilling, looked at her and
chirped. Lily chirped back, waved, and walked home.

Lily ate breakfast quickly the next day, finished her homework, stuffed her backpack full of things she thought would be useful, and walked to the big oak tree in the forest. This spot was now their official meeting place.

Lily lifted her head up high and howled like a wolf. She wasn't sure this was the correct way of calling her team, but one by one, they all showed up.

"I brought a few things that may help us," Lily said as she unpacked her bag.

They worked out every step of their plan to the smallest detail.

Lily then called upon a few more animals to help them pull this off. After explaining the plan and each animal's particular role, the day was over.

"How are you?" Lily called Eva right before going to bed that evening. "I'm sorry for not calling sooner. It's been a crazy weekend."

"That's fine; don't apologize. If I needed your help, I would've called," Eva said. "I actually went to the park with my mom yesterday. We had a picnic, played frisbee, and talked. We laughed a lot, too. That was the first time I saw her happy in a long time."

"Oh, Eva, that's wonderful."

"Yeah, it was. She had to work this morning though, so I took a walk in the woods, and you know what? At one point I heard a lot of noise. It almost sounded like an animal choir or something. And then I could have sworn I heard your voice. It was really weird. I usually don't hear anything in the woods except for a few chirps or leaves rustling but never howling, squeaking, and grunting all at the same time. I must have been hallucinating."

"Huh, that's odd, did you find out where it was coming from?" Lily hoped her secret was still safe.

"To be honest, I got scared and was all alone, so I turned around and ran home. I have no idea how you can spend hours on end in there. Don't you get scared?"

"Oh no, I love the forest. If anything, I'm more nervous in school, speaking of which, ugh, it's getting late, and we have to get up early tomorrow morning. We better get off the phone now."

"Have a good night, and thanks for calling, you really are a true friend," Eva said.

"Ditto. Sleep well. Everything will be fine. Your mom's just going through some rough times, but she loves you very much and doesn't want to disappoint you. Just remember that, okay?"

"Alright, thanks. Goodnight," Eva hung up.

Oh yeah, before I forget, I better write down everything I need for tomorrow.

When she was done, she looked over her notes and noticed she had something to do every day that week.

She then crawled into bed and immediately fell asleep and stayed asleep until the alarm clock woke her up the next morning. No dreams or nightmares. No visitors. Just much-needed sleep.

As Lily got ready for school the next morning, she pulled out her notes and stared at them.

This is actually happening. It seemed even more real to her now that she had it written on paper.

Trying to ignore this nervous feeling that was creeping up, she packed up her stuff, went downstairs, said goodbye to her parents, and walked to the bus stop.

Along the way, Viktoria came up from behind and gently pushed past Lily, giving her a mean look. Lily grunted, feeling a jabbing stab in her gut.

Viktoria stopped, turned around, and walked right up to Lily. "Is there something wrong, Missy?"

"No," Lily said.

"I don't believe you," Viktoria said. "In fact, it sounded more like you were making fun of me. That's not nice, and I want you to apologize."

"I'm sorry." Lily put her head down.

"Not accepted," Viktoria huffed. "I may accept your apology if you carry my bag to school. My shoulder still hurts because you knocked me to the ground the other day."

"I have my own bag and can't carry yours too," Lily replied in a timid voice.

"Oh, poor baby. You hurt someone else and aren't even willing to help them afterwards. Wait 'til I tell everyone at school what a horrible person you are," Viktoria promised.

"Okay, give it to me. I'll carry it until we get to the bus stop, alright?" Lily said.

"Great, here you go. Now, hurry up, or we're gonna be late," Viktoria demanded.

Viktoria walked tall and straight a few steps ahead of Lily. Lily, on the other hand, was slouched over carrying two heavy bags.

What does she put in there, rocks?

Viktoria grabbed her bag away from Lily as soon as she spotted Till. He walked over to Lily. "What was that all about?"

"She forced me to carry her bag." Lily held her head down in shame.

Till suddenly grabbed Lily by both shoulders and looked her straight in the eyes. "Lily, listen to me carefully. Don't be afraid to say no. You're strong, and I got your back! Wait right here. I'll be right back," Till stormed toward Viktoria.

"I will not watch you bully my closest friend, Viktoria," he said sternly. "This is unacceptable behavior, and you know it!

Keep your anger at home, or else you'll have to deal with me, do you understand?"

Viktoria snickered, but as soon as Till turned his back toward her, Lily noticed the look on her face. It wasn't mean or even scared. She looked sad, very, very sad.

Till returned and hugged Lily tight. He was a lot taller than her, so her ear was lying flat on his chest. She felt his heart pound. And a tingling in her body. She had butterflies in her stomach! They had hugged many, many times and she felt nothing. But this time was different.

Confused, she gently pushed away from him. "Thanks. I really appreciate it. Next time, I will say no and just walk away, I promise."

"There better not be a next time, but just in case, if you want, I can pick you up, so we can walk to the bus stop together. I'd be more than happy to do that."

"I'd really like that, thank you," Lily said.

Hhmm, that was a weird thing to say.

Normally, she would have told him not to bother since it was out of his way, but she knew she would feel safer with him by her side, and she wanted to try to understand what those butterflies were all about.

"There's Eva, come on." Till grabbed Lily's wrist and walked over to meet her.

Till started talking about his first scuba diving lesson. Eva didn't have much to say since she didn't want to talk about her mom in front of him. Lily told them she had a family weekend full of shopping, helping in the garden, watching movies, and playing board games.

Lily sighed in relief as the bus came around the corner because she felt guilty for lying and didn't want to continue. First she had lied to her parents and then to her best friends.

If this continues, I'm going to lose them!

During the whole bus ride, Lily heard whispers and felt the

cold stares of others around her. She then heard someone say, "What? Lily pushed Viktoria on the ground on purpose? Wow, Lily sure has changed since elementary school!"

But I carried her bag, why is she doing this?

"Viktoria's already started a rumor. This is going to be a rough day." Lily rolled her eyes as Till drew her near in a side hug.

Lily couldn't concentrate in class. Thoughts of suffering lab animals and Viktoria wouldn't leave her head.

Lily made sure to stay far away from her for the rest of the day. In order to do that, she had to keep a close eye on her, which wasn't fun at all.

During recess, Lily moved several times because Viktoria got too close. Finally, she passed by when Lily wasn't paying attention and threw her lunch bag on the ground at Lily's feet.

"Now you're littering, shame on you," Viktoria sneered.

By the time the last bell rang, it seemed that almost every kid in school thought Lily was a bully. *Sheesh, news spreads fast in this school.*

But not only was Lily a bad person, according to the gossip. Eva and Till were, too.

Lily spotted Till standing alone at the bus stop. Other kids from his class were there, but they stood far away from him. Lily came up to him and stood really close. As they were talking about their terrible day of whispers and mean looks, she started to lean on him.

Looking down at her, Till raised one brow, put his arm around her and kissed her head. This made Lily feel safe, and once again, the butterflies in her stomach flattered about wildly.

What is going on?

11

FOOT IN THE DOOR

After Lily got home, she spent a few minutes with her mom, telling her about her day. Everything except the part about Viktoria and the rumors. She didn't want her mom to worry. "Thanks for sharing," her mom said. "I was worried you'd just run inside, say hi, and be gone for the rest of the day like last week."

"I was just really busy last week, Mom. I'm sorry. I'll try to not do that from now on, but I do have homework, so I have to leave you now. Is that okay?"

"Of course, dear. Can't get out of homework, right?" Her mom joked.

Lily quickly went to her room, closed her door, and looked at her plan. She only had one main task to complete today.

She turned on her laptop to read about the animal testing lab in her area and then reached for the phone. A friendly voice on the other end answered.

In her deep, mature voice, Lily said, "Hi, my name is Lily Bowers. May I please speak to Dr. Schwarz?"

"May I ask why you're calling?" the receptionist asked.

"I'm working on a career project for school. I'm fascinated

by medical research, so I'd like to talk about your laboratory's achievements with the director. I want to ask if he'd be willing to schedule a short interview with me."

"He's a busy man. I'm not sure if you'll be successful, but I will put you through. One moment please."

"Dr. Schwarz here, how may I help you?"

Lily repeated her introduction and added, "In your research facility, I understand you use a combination of animal testing and alternative methods. I'd like to explore the differences between the two a little deeper. Are you willing to schedule just a few minutes of your time for an interview with me?"

"I apologize, but I don't have time right now," Dr. Schwarz replied.

"It'll only take a few minutes, and it doesn't have to be right now. I know my project won't directly benefit you or your work, but can you think of the time when you were thinking about which career path to take? Did you have anyone in this field to ask for guidance?"

"No, I didn't, but maybe it would have helped me adjust better," Dr. Schwarz sighed.

"I don't know any other lab directors and was told you're the best person to ask. Do you have just a few minutes over the next few weeks?"

"Hold on, let me check. I'm available in two weeks on Wednesday, the 27th. How about 4 pm?" he said.

"Great, 4 pm on the 27th is perfect! I'm really looking forward to meeting you in person."

They said bye and hung up.

Feeling a little guilty for making up that whole story, Lily stopped for a minute and thought about the medical field. Technically, she was interested in this field, and maybe it would be good to get to learn more about it. Either that or she was just relieving her guilt. Regardless, she didn't care. Her team's plan worked and she got in the front door.

"Whew, that went well, don't you think, Ralph? I wasn't sure if I'd actually get past the secretary, let alone get an appointment."

She used to talk to Ralph quite often, thinking she was only talking to herself, but now that she knew he could communicate with her, they were chatting all the time.

Last night, her mom heard grunts, clucks, and moans coming from her room and asked what nature documentary she was watching. Lily chuckled and told her she was learning Turtlish online to be able to speak with Ralph.

Now that the first task was completed, and she had an appointment with the lab director, worry started to settle in. And doubt. The first task just seemed too easy, and she wasn't sure what to do next.

How can I convince him to stop testing on animals? What if he throws me out as soon as he finds out I'm an animal activist and not really interested in becoming a lab director? Oh no, I shouldn't have lied!

Without wanting to waste any more time thinking about it, she forced herself back to work. After some more research, she discovered that adults really like presentations, so she looked for examples and downloaded a pretty template for free. All she had to do was replace the words and images. It sounded simple enough anyway.

But still, all she had was a just an idea at this point – an idea that sounded good but was created by a ten-year-old human and seven forest animals.

After dinner, she went back upstairs to start adding text to her presentation.

Is this even going to work? She had never created a presentation, let alone had a professional meeting with someone before. Her heart pounded like thunder.

She visualized the encounter. *Dr. Schwarz is going to laugh at me, I just know it!*

A knock on her window disrupted her thoughts. It was Alo. She was grateful that he was so quiet. Otherwise, there was no way she could let him inside while her mom was reading quietly in the next room.

"I heard about your plan, and I must say, I am impressed!" Alo said.

"Really? I'm not sure," Lily said. "I've just set up an appointment with the lab director but am sure he's going to throw me out as soon as he finds out I'm only there to save animals."

"Maybe, but if he can see the benefits he will gain, I bet he will listen."

"Yeah, maybe, but I'm not as confident as you!"

"Where is your coin?" Alo asked.

Having completely forgotten about the coin, Lily tried to remember where she left it. She fumbled through her things and finally found it in her jacket pocket.

The six hands were no longer visible. Instead, in their place was a circle. In that circle was a dead tree trunk. Next to the tree on the dry, cracked ground was a human skeleton with a crow picking at the hole where the eye used to be. On the other side, it read "To adapt is to survive, but Humans need to believe."

Alo looked at it and said, "Ah, evolution never dies. This IS good. What do you understand from this, Lily?"

Taking a few minutes to think, Lily remembered what she learned about vultures. "Animals have to adapt in order to survive. A vulture's head is featherless so that when it sticks it deep into an animal's dead body, its head won't get too dirty. Vultures even learned how to break open ostrich eggs with stones."

"Yes, that is a good example, but that's not all. What else do you see?"

"I don't know, you tell me. What do you see?" Lily asked back.

"I don't know humans as well as you, but I do know that

they are challenged with change and only seem to adapt when they don't have any other choice."

"Oh yes, I learned in a documentation film that humans have to adapt so that we all survive, but that we sometimes only adapt if we have a guarantee that we'll live a better life in the near future. We need a lot of convincing."

"Exactly. Now, when you prepare your presentation, concentrate on that main message and use your heart to find the right words and imagery," Alo said. "Also, keep an image of a healthy Mother Nature in the back of your mind. She will inspire you to do your best."

"Ah, I think I got it!" As if someone handed her the answer on a sheet of paper, she saw the way forward. "I know how to start now. Thanks for your help, Alo!"

"I will let you get to work then."

"Why don't you stay here with me, I may need you tonight."

"You'll be fine. I am sure of that. If you need me, just howl." Alo jumped off and trotted away into the dark woods.

Filled with energy, Lily wrote down her thoughts.

"Are you asleep, Lily?" Her mom knocked on the door.

"Do you think I would go to bed without saying goodnight? I've just finished my homework. Mom, can you read me a story?"

"I'd love to!"

"Let's read this." Lily grabbed a book she got for her birthday the year before but hadn't touched yet, *The Animal's Conference* by Erich Kastner.

Lily didn't think she'd ever grow out of enjoying story time. Sometimes her dad read, sometimes her mom, and sometimes she read to them. But tonight, she didn't feel like reading aloud. She just wanted to lie there quietly and listen.

Her mom read the German book long enough to get into the story, which was really, really good. Shortly after her mom and dad kissed her goodnight, Lily fell asleep.

12

THE ANIMALS HELP

After school the next day, Lily went back into the woods to meet with her team.

"Ah ouuuuuuuuuuuuu..." Her howling was getting better with practice, but she still felt silly and wondered if any forest animals secretly laughed at her.

"What?" Lily jumped when Rae, the raven, landed on her shoulder.

"Oh, it's you, you scared me!"

"Sorry, I wanted to land on that branch, but a strong wind took me straight to you instead."

The other six animals showed up one by one. Lily told them about her conversation with Dr. Schwarz. She picked up a stick and made a few drawings in the dirt to explain what she wanted to present to him.

While working out some more details, Moon, the cat, lunged at Serena, the mouse, who skittered across the path and underneath some leaves.

"Will you two please settle down!" Alpina, the wolf, scolded the duo and turned back to Lily, who looked more scared than Serena.

"It is just harmless play. At least while we are working together. We made a pact not to harm each other during this project. Nature must take its course afterward, though," Alpina explained.

What an odd party. Lily watched the animals work in perfect harmony together, not wanting to think about what would happen to the smaller animals once this was all over.

They called some more forest friends to join them for a few photos to add to the presentation, then their meeting came to an end.

The team gathered in a circle for their goodbye tradition. They all put their right paw, hand, wing or tail in the middle, one on top of the other, pushed down, and then lifted up and said, "We got this!"

With a confident smile, Lily breathed in deeply and looked deep into the vibrant forest. The colors of the leaves and small wildflowers were so bright, she could feel their positive energy.

On her way home, she saw a puffed-up baby bird sitting on the ground. Alone. Lily knelt down to ask if he needed help. The baby whimpered. The mother flew down and explained to Lily that she fell out of her nest and hurt herself.

Lily received the mother's permission to take her baby to the local vet's office. She carefully picked up the sobbing bird and walked as fast as she could.

"Hi Lily, long time, no see," the veterinarian said.

Stray baby kittens, abandoned dogs, squirrels, birds. Lily brought in many hurt animals and had become a regular at the vet's office. She even begged her mom to take her to the vet with one of those dung beetles with the blue bellies when she was three. She amused the vet so much that he framed a picture of her holding a baby squirrel and underneath engraved on a small plate on the frame, it read: "Lily Bowers, Wild Animal Caretaker."

"I found her in the woods. Can you help her?"

"Certainly." The vet carefully took the baby out of Lily's hands and examined it. "She only bruised her wing, so it'll be as good as new in a few days. She just needs to rest. Did you see any birds near her, her mother perhaps?"

"Yes, she was there. I told her I wanted you to check her out, and I would bring her right back."

Smiling wide, the vet said, "I'm sure she said 'Okay,' right? Well, go ahead and take her back. She's a fledgling, so she doesn't need to go back into her nest. Just put her in a safe place, near where you found her, where her mother was. Not in plain sight of predators or paths where people walk their dogs.

"Her mother should take care of her, but wait a while to make sure you see the mother before you leave. If she doesn't come, take the bird home with you and call the wildlife rehabilitation unit - here's their number." The vet wrote the number on a small piece of paper and handed it to Lily.

Lily knew her mother would still be there, but she took the number anyway and thanked the vet for his service once again.

Lily carefully, yet quickly, rushed the little baby back to her mama.

"There you go, sweet little girl." Lily carefully set the baby down in a safe place amongst some twigs and leaves. The mother came quickly and listened to Lily explain what the doctor said.

"I gotta go home now, but if you need my help, I live right there behind that bush. Just peck on my window. It's the far-right window on the second floor. She'll be alright though. She just needs to rest and heal."

Lily arrived home and once again felt the warmth and love right away. It must have been the Italian cooking. Spaghetti was on the menu!

Lily went up to her room after dinner to continue working on her presentation.

Her phone beeped before she could even start.

It was her friends in the group chat. After spending an hour chatting, she had no desire to work. She just talked to Ralph and then went down to watch some tv with her parents before going to bed.

I have plenty of time to finish this, no need to rush.

Over the next few days, she didn't feel like working on the presentation either. Instead, she chatted with her friends, watched tv, and hung out with Eva and Till.

One evening after dinner, she went up to her room and stared out her window into the dark forest, wondering what it'd be like to be a wolf.

"Hi Lily," Alo said after jumping on her balcony.

Startled for only a second, she said "Oh, hi," and slumbered in her chair.

"What is wrong?" he asked.

"Nothing." Lily hung her head.

"How is your presentation coming along? Are you almost finished?"

"Oh, I'm sorry, I haven't done anything with the presentation all week."

"May I ask why not?"

"I don't know. Just didn't feel like it. It's not going to work anyway. I just know it." Lily lifted up her head slowly to watch Alo's reaction.

He didn't say anything. He just sat down and stared at Lily with sad eyes.

He then stood up and walked a few steps to look at her straight in the eye.

"Lily, you are the most compassionate human I know. Remember all those animals you saved over the past few years?

You did not have any help with that. You just knew what you had to do and did it."

"My mom brought me to the vet when I was too young to go by myself. She also taught me how to pick them up carefully. I didn't do any of that alone. Why do I have to do this? I'm too young and will never be able to save Mother Nature. I'm not a superhero. I just can't do this. I'm so sorry."

"I understand, Lily. It is a huge responsibility for a young girl, and there is no guarantee that you will succeed. That can be quite demotivating."

"I knew you would understand; thanks, Alo."

"Of course, I understand. I also understand how you will feel when you succeed. I have seen you succeed and how happy you get. You motivate everyone around you with your smile and laughter. And, you are most happy when you rescue animals. The animals are most grateful when they need help and then see you because they know they can rely on you. Every animal on this planet knows about you. We are extremely lucky in Reinhardswald to physically be near you. There are thousands of animals all over this world who want to meet you. Do you realize how much you are loved?"

"Really? They love me even though they don't even know me?"

"Of course they do, Lily. You are the only one we know who has the ability to save Mother Nature. And believe me, we did not want to put this burden on you now as a young girl, so we first searched for an adult, but there is no one else like you. Your pure heart and soul are what make you special. It is why you are the chosen one."

Alo paused and watched a tear run down Lily's face.

"Close your eyes, Lily. I want you to look into the future to the point when you have completed this challenge. Picture Mother Nature with radiant healthy wings. She is happy, grateful, and full of unconditional love. Do you see her help save our beautiful Earth and all of us?"

Alo continued, "And imagine being in the middle of all the cats, mice, dogs, monkeys, and rabbits you saved. Can you see how happy and relieved they are?"

Lily nodded. And smiled.

"How do you feel now?" Alo asked after a few minutes passed.

With her eyes still closed, Lily smiled again, but no words came out.

"Ooo," Lily shook her head and arms, as it felt like a prickly porcupine rolling up and down the right side of her body.

She opened her eyes and looked intently at Alo, saying, "I understand now. I can't disappoint them." Lily lowered her head again.

"You cannot disappoint yourself, Lily. That is more important. You are happiest when you save animals, are you not?"

"Yes, I guess I am." Lily sat on her bed.

Alo walked to her and put his head on her shoulder. Holding him tight, Lily started to cry.

"What if I fail? What if Mother Nature dies? It'll be all my fault."

"No, that is where you are wrong. It would not be your fault. No one is to blame, Lily."

"So, no animal would be mad at me if I fail?" Lily asked timidly.

"Why would we be mad? We know you will do your best, and we are here to help. How can we get mad about that?

"But regardless, Lily, why are you constantly talking about failing? I would not have walked into your room the very first time we met if I thought you were going to fail.

"Mother Nature would not have exposed herself to you either. Nor would any animal or tree have communicated with you. Although we cannot predict the future, we know you will succeed. There is not a doubt in our minds!"

"Do you really think I can save Mother Nature?" Lily's eyes got really big in anticipation of Alo's answer.

"I do not think you will succeed, Lily, I know it."

Over the next few days, Lily worked hard to perfect her presentation.

She was super grateful for Ralph, the best assistant ever. Not only did he offer intelligent suggestions, but he also made her feel like she wasn't alone and helpless.

Her jittery nerves relaxed when he was sitting on her desk, inspecting everything she did. She certainly didn't mind having him look over her pencil. Once, he even made a joke while correcting her grammar.

A few days passed by quickly, and before she knew it, it was the night before her meeting with Dr. Schwarz.

She put the final touches on her presentation after school, then went into the woods to show her team.

"That is beautiful, Lily, you did a wonderful job!" Alpina spoke first. The others nodded in agreement.

At that moment, Mother Nature appeared. "Lily, we are very grateful for your help. You created an amazing presentation, and I'm confident you will succeed. You are our shining light in this dark forest!"

Lily beamed with joy, but then doubt kicked in once again. "But what if I fail? What if Dr. Schwarz turns me away?"

Mother Nature opened her wings wide and looked up to the sky. The trees around started to shake and rattle, and a beam of sunlight shone down on Lily. "You will succeed in the end, my dear. Do not worry."

But Lily did worry and barely slept that night.

13

THE BIG MEETING

At the end of the school day, Lily took a different bus to go to Dr. Schwarz' office. While she was reviewing her notes, she felt heat move from her wobbly stomach up to her face, and her jittery hands caused the paper to rattle so much that she couldn't read anymore.

It took all of her strength to stand up and get off the bus. Once she got to the building, she stood in front of the door, trying to gain enough courage to walk through it.

While contemplating whether to walk through the door or run away, a sparrow flew up to a branch near her. "Good luck and thank you, Lily! We are so proud of you. You will do a great job!" Lily smiled and walked through the door.

"I'm here to see Dr. Schwarz," she said to the woman at the front desk.

The receptionist looked up and asked curiously, "And you are?"

"Lily Bowers."

The receptionist looked at her calendar. "Please wait over there. I'll ring him now."

As Lily waited, she noticed a magazine on the table. There

was a monkey in a cage, and the caption read, "We Are All Monkeys In Cages."

She read the article. It was about an experiment in 1967 of five monkeys who were put in a cage with a ladder. On the top was a bunch of bananas. Immediately, one monkey climbed the ladder to get to the bananas. But before he could reach them, he got sprayed with cold water. Startled, he climbed back down. But not only that, then the other four monkeys also got sprayed with cold water.

After a few minutes, another monkey climbed up the ladder, and the same thing happened. When this happened a third time, the monkey who climbed not only got sprayed with cold water, he also got beaten by the other four.

One monkey was then replaced by a new monkey, who spotted the bananas and — unaware of the situation — climbed the ladder but immediately got beaten by the other four monkeys. This repeated when a second monkey was replaced and tried to climb the ladder to grab the bananas.

All five monkeys were eventually replaced with new monkeys who never found out why they were beaten or why they attacked the one trying to climb the ladder. As far as they knew, that was how things worked there and so they must comply.

The article went on to explain how humans work in the same way. Sometimes, employees have new ideas but are shot down quickly by management, and if this happens too often, eventually no one will try new things anymore and the employees will either remain silent or leave to find a better opportunity where their voices will be heard.

Hhmm, sad that they have to cage monkeys to figure this out about human nature. Makes no sense.

"Lily Bowers?" a tall man wearing black, thick-rimmed glasses said in a deep voice.

"Yes ... Dr. Schwarz?" she asked timidly.

"I must say, I was expecting an older teenager, not a young school girl, but I'm still very happy to meet you. Please, come this way."

His long white lab coat swayed back and forth as they walked through a wide white corridor. Everything was white: the walls, doors, floors, desks, clothes, absolutely everything. There were also many rooms with bolted doors on both sides.

Once they entered Dr. Schwarz's office, Lily took out the presentation from her bag.

She stalled with small talk, then dove into why she was really there. "I am very interested in medical research and do believe I'd be a wonderful lab technician or maybe a director someday because I want to help people. But I must be honest with you that I'd only pursue this career if things were done differently.

"You see, I live in the magical forest, Reinhardswald. It's my sacred home and the home to many wild animals. Recently, I met Mother Nature, who asked for my help. You may think I imagined this, but it's the truth. She spoke of how humans tortured animals for our benefit. I knew about animal testing, and my mom does everything she can to buy products that are cruelty-free, but sometimes, it's impossible. Sometimes, we have no choice, such as with medicine.

"Did you know that many tests were reported as useless, absolutely useless?"

"Yes, I knew that," Dr. Schwarz replied with a sorry smile.

"The European ban on animal testing in the cosmetic industry in 2013 helped," Lily continued, "but that's just for the end product in one industry and in one region of this big Earth. There are so many more industries and countries who don't seem to have any plans in the near future to stop."

Lily started to tear up. *Breathe, Lily, breathe.*

"I know we can't change the law in other countries, but we can make changes here in Germany and in Europe. If we're successful, we can inspire other countries with our positive example."

"If we continue causing harm to animals, we'll all suffer and won't be able to recover. Mother Nature is very sick, and if she can no longer take care of the plants and animals on our sacred Earth, everything around us will die, including humans. The forest will become a cold and barren cemetery. There will be no plants to provide us with oxygen. The mountains will become bald, hills barren, and the rivers and lakes will dry up. It'll look like this."

She handed him a photo of dead cats and mice lying on the ground in the forest.

They were not dead though. The cats and mice were only playing dead when they took that photo two weeks prior. But Dr. Schwarz couldn't tell the difference. He didn't act shocked though either as he flicked the photo on the table in front of Lily.

Lily then showed him photos of the dead trees and barren parts of the forest. She found these areas in the deep part of the woods, off the beaten path. The lab director raised his eyebrows but still didn't say anything.

When she showed him a close-up photo of Mother Nature's wing with barely a feather on it, she looked him straight in the eye and said in a low voice, "These photos represent the destruction that will soon be reality."

"Ms. Bowers, let me stop you right here. I am aware of the harm done to animals. And I know there are alternative methods. I use these methods too, but we must continue to test on animals for the safety of humans. I understand your compassion for animals though. I love them too. But, I honestly don't believe testing will ruin our planet, and even if it were the case, I'm not able to change anything, nor do I have the time or energy to spend time on it. Much less the desire."

"I understand that your time is limited, Dr. Schwarz. But, if you completely stop animal testing in your lab, you'll set an example for others."

"We stopped testing on cosmetics once the ban was in effect, but the medical industry is a completely different story," he said. "I can't change that, no matter how much I'd like to. Or, do you have a suggestion?"

Lily could tell he was getting a little annoyed with her.

"Just like with anything else. If you want something bad enough, you work hard to get it. You can work together with your colleagues and demand change within the medical industry. If you remain silent and accept the law as it is, nothing will change. But if you voice your opinion and go public, people will listen."

Surprised by her quick wit, Dr. Schwarz raised his eyebrows again and chuckled, "You are absolutely correct, but it doesn't change the fact that this takes a lot of time. Time that I just don't have. I'm sorry, Lily, but I have to get back to work now. I really appreciate your visit and am thrilled to have met your acquaintance. I wish you much luck. I'm sure you'll move mountains along your career path!"

He got up from his desk and motioned for Lily to get up and leave. She sadly put her stuff in her bag and slowly stood up. "Thank you for your time, Dr. Schwarz. I really appreciate it." He escorted her to the door.

Standing alone outside of the huge cold, white building, Lily felt the weight of her heavy bag on her shoulders. Frustrated, she yanked it off and threw it on the ground. Her knees collapsed on top of her bag. Her body felt warm again as tears started to form in her eyes. She sobbed silently, then got up and walked to the bus stop.

While waiting on the bench, an old woman in a black cloak sat down beside her. Her many deep wrinkles and frizzy, white, tangled hair kind of reminded Lily of her great-grandmother who recently passed away. Lily used to sit with her for hours, just listening to her tell stories of her past. Usually World War II stories but seen from the perspective of a nine-year-old child living in Germany. Her Omi (as Lily called her) talked about how grateful she had been for the things she had then, which wasn't much.

A meal with meat was pure luxury and a sign of prosperity, but they only had it once a week if they were lucky. Omi also told stories of how the American soldiers would give her and her friends handouts. A potato or piece of candy.

One kind soldier even handed her a book, *The Wonderful Wizard of Oz* by L. Frank Baum. She couldn't read it because it was in English, but as soon as she collected enough money, she bought the translated German version in a local bookstore and devoured it over a weekend. She gave both versions to Lily right before her death. Lily stayed up reading them with her flashlight under the covers as a thank you memorial to her Omi after she passed away.

Sniff, sniff. Lily's nose was getting congested as tears started to fall down her face.

The old woman hummed softly, which calmed Lily down. The song was one that Omi used to sing to Lily at night. It was the German nursery rhyme, "Schlaf, Kindlein, Schlaf" which meant "Sleep, Little Child, Sleep." Lily joined in and started to hum along. The woman smiled, and they hummed together until the bus came.

Lily got lost in her thoughts of her Omi while riding the bus. Lily felt a faint tap on her shoulder. She looked up and saw the kind eyes of the old woman who motioned to look at the sign in the front of the bus. It was Lily's stop! She had to get off!

14

FACING THE TEAM

While getting off the bus, Lily noticed that the old woman was getting off too. They nodded at each other and went in different directions.

Lily couldn't have walked any slower. She didn't want to have to tell her team of new friends that she failed. It was too late to tell them tonight though. She'd have to wait until tomorrow.

"Boo!" Till jumped in front of Lily, blocking her way.

"Oh, stop that, you scared me!" She was happy to see him but too sad to show it.

"Everything alright?" he asked.

"Yeah, I'm just a bit sad, that's all."

"Why, what's wrong?"

"Just a bad day at school, that's all. Everything will be fine," she replied.

"Well, okay, if you say so, Lil."

The hair on Lily's arms stood at attention. She loved it when he called her Lil. "I'm fine, really. Thanks for asking. Middle school is just a lot different than elementary school. I miss my old school."

"I hear you. It took me almost a whole year to get used to it. But now that I'm in the seventh grade, it's gotten a lot easier. Not the homework or the tests though. I can tell this year is going to be the hardest one EVER!"

"Ugh, sorry to hear that. But you're a smart guy, so you can handle it."

Till's cheeks turned red. He knew he was smart. In fact, he was a genius and tutored ninth graders in biology and math! But every time Lily reminded him, he got embarrassed.

"Thanks. Okay, here you are, home sweet home. Tell your parents I said 'Hi.' Have a good night. See you tomorrow!" And off he went.

The next few days were a bit troubling for Lily. Not only did she feel guilty for not convincing Dr. Schwarz, she felt horrible for not going into the woods and telling her team what happened.

Ralph tried to encourage her to go, but she just couldn't do it. She couldn't bear to see their disappointed faces. Regardless of what Alo told her.

On their way home from school, Eva and Till asked Lily to go to the indoor skating rink with them. "No, I have some homework to finish, and I don't want to have to deal with it over the weekend. But have fun," Lily replied quietly.

While walking home, she passed the same old lady with a black cloak whose humming soothed her after the failed presentation.

"Oh, hello there, sweet girl, how are you today?" the old lady asked.

"I'm fine, just a little sad, but I'll be okay." Lily raised her eyebrow, surprised that she revealed her sadness to a complete stranger.

The lady stopped walking, pulled off her hood, and turned to look at Lily.

Her bright sparkling green eyes had the mesmerizing power to stop even a snake from biting.

"It's okay to be sad, my dear," the old lady said. "You can't be happy all the time because if you were, you wouldn't appreciate being happy. Just remember, you have many friends all around you who are there for you, cheering you on, whether you succeed or fail. They're forgiving and love you no matter what."

"Do you really think that's true?" Lily asked.

"I've been around longer than you can imagine. I don't think that's true. I know it's true!"

Lily sighed and smiled at her. "Thank you. I'd love to walk home with you the rest of the way, but I have something very important to take care of. I hope to see you again though."

"I would really like that. Take care of yourself," the old lady said as Lily walked away.

Lily didn't even stop home to drop off her bag. She walked straight into the forest and texted her mom that she'd be home a little later.

"Aaaaaaaoooooooouuuuuuuu."

Within less than a minute, her team was assembled in front of her with eager looks on their faces. Lily apologized for waiting so long. She also told them how scared she was to admit her failure.

"Why do you think you failed, Lily?" the fox asked. "We did not expect you to change the world in a day. It takes time, lots of it, and we have only just begun. And you will stumble and fall along the way. Just like we all do. We all fail." The animals all nodded with him in agreement.

He continued, "Do you know how many tries it takes for me to catch a rabbit? Sometimes I have to come home without any food for my family, and I feel horrible. But that does not stop me from trying again the following day."

"But my goal was to get this lab to stop testing on animals. I wasted my time on this stupid presentation. I wasted your time on thinking out a plan. All for nothing. And to be honest, I have no clue what to do now," Lily confessed.

"Neither do we, but that is okay because we will figure this out together. Tell us about your meeting," Sam, the owl, cooed.

Lily explained everything she said to Dr. Schwarz and why he wasn't willing to help.

Trixi, the deer, interrupted. "So, let me get this straight, even though he would like to see change, he is not willing to do anything about it. It sounds like he is just plain lazy."

"He said he didn't have the time or energy. I hear many adults say that," Lily said.

"That lab director sounds like a tough nut, and one that we are not going to crack today," Rae chirped. "And from what you have just said, Lily, others will feel the same way. This is going to be a challenge. Let us meet next Saturday. This should give us enough time to gather our thoughts and think of a new plan."

"I will consult with Alo while we take turns caring for Mother Nature," Alpina said.

"Caring for Mother Nature? What's wrong?" Lily gasped.

"She is very weak now. The seasons are changing, which makes her most vulnerable. Her leaves are starting to turn a different color, and soon they will all fall off. She may not have the strength to handle the cold winter that follows. This will be her first winter without enough feathers to keep her warm."

"What can I do to help?" Lily asked.

"Just send her your love and keep hope in your heart," replied Alpina. "We have to protect her, and the only way to do that is being by her side, sharing stories and memories and showing our pure unconditional love and devotion."

"Oh, I understand. I actually wanted to see her today to tell her what happened," Lily said sadly.

"She already knows." Alo sat down in front of Lily. "You may not have realized it, but she was with you the entire time."

"Is she upset with me?"

"Certainly not. She is very proud of you. She cannot come now, but you will see her again soon. I am also very proud of you. From what I heard, you put on one amazing presentation, and I am convinced you left a mark on the heart of that lab director."

Alo stood very tall and held his head so high that he was as tall as Lily. "Now, come, let us walk." He nudged her away from the small crowd, who quickly scattered off in different directions.

"You know, Lily, if I did not know any better, I would not have thought you were a human. With your wisdom, charm, and mannerisms, you are more like a wolf to me. I would accept you in my family any day!" Alo's voice cracked.

Lily looked at him and noticed a small drop of water running down his face.

Can wolves even cry?

"There have been a few humans who were accepted in wolf families over time but not many. We are scared of most humans. But not you. You stop to observe the beauty of nature. You appreciate the magic of this forest. You spend time to take care of hurt animals in need, even if it is just a beetle. It is also rare to find humans who clearly and respectfully communicate with everyone."

"Oh, but I know many humans who do all that too," Lily replied. "My parents taught me to be kind and respectful to every living being."

"Yes, I know. They taught you well."

They stopped at the hedge to Lily's backyard, and he turned toward her. "Please remember to look at the coin again tonight." Alo must have known she forgot about it more than once. "If you need me, just howl, and I will come. Goodnight."

Lily smiled and walked home. Her happy thoughts turned to sadness when she envisioned Mother Nature in a weak state. *Changing seasons, cold winter, no feathers? How will she survive winter? Can Mother Nature really die?*

Many thoughts and questions invaded Lily's mind. And there was nothing she wanted more than to be able to save her. But she needed to help her soon though, before winter break. It was now the end of September. Only two more months before it got really cold.

Lily, Eva, and Till spent Saturday morning together at the local park. Autumn leaves whizzed all around them as they deeply inhaled the brisk September air.

Something about fall energized Lily. How nature charmingly prepared itself for a deep sleep before sprouting new life once again.

Jumping in huge piles of dry leaves became a part of her daily routine. But only when the leaves were dry. Wet leaves were kind of icky.

And then there was Halloween, her favorite day of the year! Designing a costume and getting dressed up. Having Mom put crazy makeup on her and walking around the neighborhood scaring anyone who opened the door. When else could you have so much fun? Not to mention all the candy!

Halloween was a bit different in the States though. She remembered wearing cute outfits like a ladybug or a princess' dress. Of course, she was younger then, but still, costumes were scarier in Germany, even for young children. There was no such thing as a cute Halloween costume because the point of Halloween was to scare off the evil spirits, not to attract them with cuteness. The most common outfits were zombies, werewolves, and even murderers, which freaked her out at first, but not anymore.

"I'm dressing up as a mummy this year." Eva turned to Lily with a hopeful look for approval.

"Oh yeah, a mummy's good. I think I'll go as a deer zombie this year and hang around the pet cemetery, muah ha. What about you?" Lily asked Till.

"I'm dressing up as a tornado that blows everyone's house down."

"Now how are you going to do that?" Eva sneered.

"I've got it all figured out. It's really not that difficult, just gotta be a little creative."

15

ALMOST TOO MUCH ANIMALISH

Scuffling their feet over the dried leaves, Till suggested they leave the park and go to his house. In unison, the two girls squealed with delight.

Till's backyard was more like an amusement park. He had a climbing wall, a fifty-meter tire zipline, a basketball hoop, two soccer goals on each end, and other fun garden games.

His mom inherited a large piece of land where they took care of three pigs, two cows, and five chickens they rescued from horrible conditions as well as maintained a large garden full of fruits and vegetables.

Lily loved when Till came over with a basket full of whatever: apples, snap beans, corn on the cob, tomatoes, etc. Their strawberries and blueberries were the best, and Till would always make those trips extra special.

One time, he dressed up as Little Red Riding Hood and asked if the Big Bad Wolf was inside eating his grandmother. Lily's dad choked from laughing so hard. Till not only got an invite for dinner that evening, Lily's dad dressed up like a squirrel and delivered a basket of fresh walnuts from their tree to Till and his family a few weeks later.

At Till's house, they only ate what they made themselves or bought from a local organic farm. Till never ate the cafeteria food either. He got something to drink but always brought a packed lunch, which looked and most likely tasted better than what she ate for lunch at school.

Her grumbling tummy reminded her she had not eaten since early that morning. But it wasn't time to eat yet; it was time to play.

"Come on you two, let's zipline. Hey, where's your dog?" Lily asked.

"She's here somewhere. Nala, Nala, come here girl!"

Out of the bushes charged a chocolate lab, who stopped right in front of Till, tongue hanging out, huffing and puffing with her googly eyes wide open that always seemed to say, "Feed ME!"

"Good girl! Go get your ball," Lily said in a burst of laughter, watching Nala look frantically for her ball.

"She's so silly, how old is she now?"

"Four years going on six months. She's a sweetheart, but a nut job sometimes. Gotta love her though."

"I wish I had a dog or a cat. But I'm grateful I have Ralph, even though he's not that cuddly."

"I love Ralph!" Eva cut in. "I wish I was allowed to have a pet, but my mom won't allow it. She's allergic to cats, doesn't have time for a dog, and doesn't know how to take care of anything else. She says we don't have time. But I have a lot of time to take care of a pet."

"You can always play with Nala when you want. Let's zipline now!" Till rushed to the tire and, with a giant leap, hopped on and flew down the tethered rope. Nala sprinted after him, ball still in her mouth and ready to play catch.

For the next hour or so, they ziplined, threw some hoops, and played a little soccer, though the girls only played soccer to humor Till.

"Lunch is ready!" Till's mom shouted from the terrace.

Feeling her heart explode, Lily stopped in mid-swing and ran so fast toward the house that she tripped over Mia, Till's cat, who was stretched out and napping on the porch.

Startled by her clumsiness, Lily meowed. "I'm sorry, Mia, please forgive me."

"It's okay, I love the food here too and run to get it without paying attention as well," Mia laughed.

"What did you say? It sounded like you were having a conversation with Mia," Till's mom interrupted.

Stumbling for an explanation, Lily replied, "Oh, nothing, I just apologized to Mia for tripping over her."

Feeling relieved his mom didn't question her further, she walked carefully but briskly to the table. Almost drooling, the three of them stared at their plates. What a meal! Homemade pot pie!

Everything tasted so much better at Till's house. Not that her parents couldn't cook, but Till's mom was, without a doubt, the best cook she knew.

Following the best pot pie Lily had ever tasted, they continued to play until it was time to go home for dinner.

It was pizza night, and she didn't want to be late for that!

As she scarfed down the first slice, Lily asked, "Mom, can we start buying food from the same organic farm Till does?"

"We've been through this a dozen times, dear. We are not Till's parents and don't have the money or the time to cook like his mom. I know she's a master cook, and I'm sorry to disappoint you, but we're doing the best we can."

"I know, but it's really not that much more money. You always talk about the quality of things. The food just tastes SO much better. And the animals are treated better at organic farms too. Please, pretty please."

"Lily, NO. That's enough; eat your pizza and be happy."

Lily felt her mom's glare and kept her head down for the rest of the meal.

The Bowers family played a card game that night. They even made popcorn and watched an animated movie, but Lily wasn't into it. Still annoyed by her mom's reaction at the dinner table, Lily rolled off the couch after the movie was over, said goodnight, and trudged upstairs.

As she was brushing her teeth, she noticed Ralph was on her nightstand next to her coin, staring at it. "Come here, Lily, I am getting a weird feeling about this coin. I think it is about to change or something," he said.

Oh no! Lily forgot to look last night after Alo told her to. Rushing over, she examined the coin closely. The circle of hands was showing again, so apparently it changed since the last time she saw it, but whew, it was nothing new! She definitely couldn't afford to miss anything.

"Something is happening," Ralph squealed.

Watching intensely, Lily saw the coin slowly morph from the circle of hands to a trophy. She turned it around and read it to Ralph out loud: "Winning only comes to those who participate."

"Hmm, well, duh, that's obvious." Rolling her eyes, Lily put the coin down and crawled into bed.

"Wake up, wake up. We want to get an early start." Lily's mom gently shook her shoulder.

Lily's parents bought a canoe a few years before with the intention of taking a canoe trip at least once a month. They didn't always go, but today the sun beamed perfectly for such a trip.

When they docked along the riverbed to eat lunch, Lily jumped out to get the canoe over a shallow area and noticed a small fish stuck between two pieces of rock on the bottom. She moved the rocks to free him.

"You're welcome," Lily blubb-blubbed to the fish who let out a meek, "thank you."

"What did you say?" Lily's dad lifted his left brow.

"I just said 'you're welcome' to the fish I rescued."

"It sounded more like 'Blubb, blubb, blubb' to me. Were you speaking Fishish?" her dad chuckled.

Lily laughed, realizing how insane that must have sounded.

Whew, I better be more careful.

This was the first time her parents had caught her talking to an animal other than Ralph.

That wasn't the only time during that trip though.

Lily whistled, "Good morning," to a pigeon flying over her head, but she didn't think her parents really noticed because Lily often whistled.

But then, she almost stepped on a frog while getting out of the canoe. His warning was loud enough for all to hear. Lily apologized profusely. Her parents stopped in their tracks and just glared at her. Seeing their faces, Lily immediately stopped and nervously dismissed it as being her silly self.

"What on earth is going on, Lily? All day, you've been making really weird noises. Are you getting sick or do you just need to pass some gas? We're family, go ahead, let it all out!" her dad laughed.

Lily loved how her dad often saved her from awkward situations. Even though farting wasn't exactly something Lily wanted to be associated with, she knew he wouldn't ever say that in front of others.

"You're the best, Dad—you know that?" Lily gave him a big hug. "Go ahead, squeeze all the gas out of me!"

Paddling along the peaceful river, the only sound that filled the river bed was the choir of birds and the soft splashes of fish jumping to catch the insects flying above the water.

"I wish we could do this every weekend," Lily sighed.

"We do too, dear." Her mom stroked her hair.

"Hey, check out that tree! It almost looks like an angel smiling at us." Dad pointed at a big willow tree with long wavy branches cascading just above the surface of the water.

As they acknowledged its beauty, a gust of wind separated the branches, inviting them inside its sheltered cave. Feeling a bolt of energy run down her arms, Lily paddled inside. Time stood still while they sat in silence, hypnotized by the waving strands of willow hair.

She felt a tickling sensation on her neck and found a strand of willow caught in her hair. She gently pulled it out. But it didn't fall where she cast it. The strand stayed in midair and slowly fluttered down to the riverbed, where a faint light shone in the water.

The light surfaced to the top, transforming to what looked like a face. Mother Nature's face smiled wide at Lily. Lily smiled back.

Her smile quickly faded once she remembered she wasn't alone. Gritting her teeth, she slowly turned around only to see her parents weren't paying attention at all. They were leaning on each other with their eyes closed.

Whew, that was close.

But when she turned around to see Mother Nature again, she was gone and so was the light. The willow strand was swaying back and forth along the river's surface again.

A dragonfly whizzed past her head and hummed, "It's SO nice to meet you, Lily. Thanks for all your help!"

Calmness entered her body as she laid her head in her

mom's lap, closed her eyes, and enjoyed the gentle back and forth rocking of the canoe.

"Wake up." Lily's mom gently massaged her head. "We all fell asleep, and now it's time to head home."

Lily looked at her watch, and it was three o'clock. They had been sleeping there for over an hour.

They paddled to their destination and drove home in peaceful silence.

16

FIND YOUR PASSION

The family ate dinner, and then Lily went up to her room exhausted. Ralph eagerly came out of his shell to hear about Lily's trip. He listened to her story of the communication slips with the other animals, the invitation of the willow tree, and the vision of Mother Nature.

"You know, Lily, I have tried many times to talk to you in the past, but you never understood me. I would ask to be put on your desk while you did your homework, but you brought me into your bathroom sink to drink water. And once I asked for some dandelions, and instead, you put me in the pond to swim. Eventually, I stopped talking and just concentrated on my thoughts. That seemed to work better.

"Remember the time when you were studying for a math test in third grade and asked me how to solve that one multiplication exercise? I knew the answer but wanted you to figure it out yourself, so I sent you my thoughts. Three minutes later, you jumped up and solved the problem."

"Really? I had no idea! Wait, so when Dad brought you home as a 'Welcome to Germany' gift for me, you were trying to talk to me? I remember you made a lot of noise when you were a little baby, but I thought it was normal for a tortoise. And when I asked my parents to listen, you never made a peep."

"Yes, I was told to not talk in front of your parents, so I kept my beak shut when they were around. When we were alone, just the two of us, I tried to tell you that your dad rescued me from the dangers of a busy street. My previous owner apparently did not want me anymore and set me out on the curb, but shortly after, your dad found me and brought me to you.

Unfortunately, I wasn't able to explain all that. Only gibber jabber came out of my mouth instead of words. I was just a baby, and you were only six years old yourself."

Intrigued by this new information, Lily started to remember other incidents in the past when they talked. They shared more memories of communication breakdowns and also of their dreams. And fears.

"I just want to live in a world without animal abuse. Is that so hard? I mean, this has been going on forever! I can't even get my mom to buy organic food. How am I supposed to convince people to not test on animals? How can I save animals and Mother Nature?"

Lily sighed heavily. "I know now that it doesn't have to do with age, and I also know that I have friends to help me, but still, this won't be easy, and I'm already tired of the fight. I just want it all to go away."

Ralph lowered his head and didn't speak. Lily thought he was falling asleep until he raised his head and stretched as close to Lily as he could. "Close your eyes and imagine yourself in ten years. Look at Mother Nature. Is she alive and well? How are the animals around you? Are they happy, free, and being well taken care of? What do you want the world to look like in ten years?"

A broad smile appeared on Lily's face as she saw a world where all animals were healthy and happy.

"Just keep that thought in your head for now."

"It's a great thought, but it's a dream. I still don't know how to make it come true."

"Maybe you'll figure it out in your dreams. Now go to bed. You have school in the morning, and I am exhausted. I need to go to sleep," Ralph demanded.

On the way to their first class the next morning, Lily tripped over Eva while trying to look at a poster.

"Hey, be careful!" Eva followed her gaze to see the new poster in the hallway. The title read, "Find Your Passion," and it said all students were invited to enter.

There would be a contest held in November, in which nominated students would present an idea that would make a positive change in the world and that they felt passionate about.

The winner would be invited to Berlin to present their idea to the German parliament to try to get support from the government and initiate political change.

"That's it!" Lily said out loud.

"What's it? What are you talking about?" Eva asked.

"I'm going to enter this contest, and if I win, I may be able to stop animal testing in Germany for good!" she replied.

"Animal testing?" Till asked. "Since when did you become an animal rights activist?"

"Since I found out what they do to innocent animals. It breaks my heart."

Lily explained how she'd been researching the past few weeks about cruel experiments and even told them about her visit with the director at the laboratory.

"I think that's a wonderful idea. Go for it," Eva said. "If you need any help, I'm here for you. I'm not really sure what I could do, but I don't think it's right to harm animals either."

"I'd be more than happy to help too," Till said. "The other week, I watched a documentary with my parents about false labeling, and we realized that some of the products we've bought that claimed to be cruelty-free actually do tests on animals. My mom was furious and wrote each company but still hasn't received an answer yet."

The last bell rang. "We better go, but let's talk about this later. I have some ideas and could really use help with this. Thanks so much!"

They met at Lily's house after school. She showed them her presentation and talked about the meeting with the lab director.

Eva and Till stared at each other, surprised by the amount of work Lily completed behind their backs. Usually, they talked about everything, so they couldn't understand why Lily kept this a secret.

"I'm sorry, but I didn't think you'd understand," Lily confessed.

"Are you kidding me? I'm no animal rights activist, but you know how much I care about animals," Till said. "But it doesn't matter now. We couldn't have helped change the lab director's mind anyway. He's just doing what he's paid to do. We all need to stop buying products that are tested on animals. There are plenty of cruelty-free products out there."

"That seems like a really hard thing to do, though, don't you think?" Eva asked.

"Not really, just takes a bit of research to find the right products. What makes it difficult is to change people's thinking, but what if we motivate just one person? That one person may be able to motivate another person. You may not change everyone's minds overnight, but if you're able to change one person's perspective, the rippling effect could be pretty amazing," Till replied.

"Your presentation is really good, but I know how we can

make it even better. What if we made a video instead of just showing photos? I have a decent video camera and can add some computer graphics to spice it up a bit," Till said.

"My mom knows someone who volunteers at an animal rights organization. Maybe she has some real live footage of what goes on in these labs. I'll ask her!" Eva said.

"Oh wow, that'd be incredible, thanks so much." Lily felt grateful and relieved her friends were willing to help. Her animal team was super, but when it came down to working on the computer, they were pretty useless.

When her friends left, Lily sat down at her desk and stared at the photo of the dead cats lying on the ground she took in the forest. Luckily her friends didn't ask her where that photo came from because she didn't have an answer ready.

Lily thought it would be good to add footage about current tests. But what about the future? She wanted to show how life would be in several decades if this abuse were to continue. If Mother Nature died or was no longer able to watch over all life on Earth anymore.

With the photo of the dead animals, it was easy for her to get the shot because she had asked her forest friends to lie still without moving. But how could Till make a video of a dead forest if she didn't tell him the whole truth? She still really wanted their help but was afraid to tell them too much because surely, they would laugh at her.

A low grumbling sound of thunder abruptly disrupted her thoughts. Looking up out onto her backyard, she noticed a faint glow moving ever so slowly across the lawn.

What looked like a ghost in the distance became clearer as it approached Lily. Her weak and withering appearance brought Lily to tears.

"I am sorry to upset you, sweet Lily. It is not my intention, but I wanted to visit you tonight to tell you that it is time to tell your friends about me," Mother Nature whispered in a meek voice.

"I now believe they will understand, and it will only make your job easier. I trust them. Meet me in the forest tomorrow and bring your friends. And the video camera."

"Really? But what if they laugh at me and think I'm crazy?" Lily asked.

"I do not think that of them. They want to help too, and I believe it would be a good idea for you to let them," Mother Nature replied.

"Thank you so much! Um, can you read my mind too?" Lily asked.

"Only when I need to," Mother Nature said and silently glided out over Lily's balcony and into the darkness without disappearing into sparkles or anything.

Lily's tears streamed down her face.

She breathed slowly and deeply to calm herself down so that she could text Eva and Till about meeting in the forest tomorrow.

"I'll be there and hey, guess what? My mom's friend said that it shouldn't be a problem to use some video clips, but that she had to check and will get back to me later this week," Eva texted back.

Till replied, "With bells on and camera in hand. Good job, Eva!"

Whew, at least I don't have to sneak around them anymore.

Ralph also let out a sigh of relief because he really had a difficult time remaining silent when Eva was around. She was his favorite human next to Lily.

Oh wow, they're gonna totally freak out when they meet her! And Alo!

The following day was a holiday. It was October 3rd, Germany Unity Day. After sleeping in and having a long, relaxing breakfast with her family, Eva and Till came to pick up Lily.

Lily stopped in front of the bush with the little hole leading to her forest. Taking a deep breath, she asked Eva and Till if they were ready for a magical experience.

"Whatever, just go, we're right behind you," Till replied impatiently.

"Hello, Lily!" It was the little baby bird she took to the vet the other week.

"Oh, hello, you look perfectly well now," Lily chirped back as the baby bird flew away.

Raising his brow, Till nudged Eva and chuckled.

Lily noticed the trees swaying back and forth as they walked past, almost as if they were welcoming her friends. One feisty little tree leaned over and touched Eva on her head. Eva didn't even realize it though. Lily looked up, shook her head, and smiled.

"Let's stop here," Lily said, sitting on a flat rock at the river bank.

She motioned for Eva and Till to sit down with her. "Today, you'll meet a few of my new friends, but please don't be afraid. They're now your friends, too, and are here to help us. They need our help to survive."

"What the?" Till stood up straight, teeth clenched and eyes wide open. He looked like he was ready to fight.

17

THE ENCHANTED FOREST

Lily looked in the direction Till was staring and saw Alo creeping through the thick shrubs surrounding the trees.

"Um, that's a wolf coming our way. Stay calm because they sense fear." Till slowly bent down to grab a thick stick lying on the ground and waved it around to try to scare him off. Eva was frozen solid.

Alo slowly walked closer and rolled his eyes at Lily.

"Till, put the stick down and meet Alo. Show him a little respect. He's been helping me over the past few weeks. He's my friend."

Till kept his death grip on the stick.

Lily breezed past Till to greet Alo. Bending forward, she grit her teeth to let Alo sniff. Then she turned to see Till brandishing the stick the way her mom told her to if she ever saw a wild boar.

"Stop it! Are you insane, Till? Please, calm down!" Lily pleaded.

But Till didn't.

"Seriously, it's okay!" Lily said a bit more fiercely. She turned to Alo. "Don't mind him, he's just being protective."

"I did not expect anything else, to be honest," Alo muttered.
Lily walked back to Till and put her hand on the stick. He
softened his grip, and she threw it aside. Then, she took his
hand and escorted him to meet Alo.

Alo bowed his head before Till and sat down. Till bowed
his head, keeping his fierce, wide-opened eyes on Alo.

Lily looked over to Eva, who was still shaking. She looked
like she was contemplating walking over to them or running far
away.

"It's okay, Eva, come here. Trust me; he's as sweet as Till's
lab," Lily said.

Eva cautiously walked over. Without really knowing what to
do, she clumsily knelt before Alo so that she could greet him
eye to eye. Alo slowly moved his head forward to smell her
mouth, causing her to lean back, shaking.

Lily explained that wolves greet each other by smelling
teeth. In a quiet giggle, Eva moved forward and opened her
mouth wide.

"Mother Nature is not feeling well today but still wants to
meet your friends. She can't stay for long though. She needs
her rest," Alo told Lily.

"I'm so sorry. I hope we can save her in time." Lily lowered
her head.

Feeling the confused stares of Eva and Till, Lily realized
what had just happened. She turned to Eva and Till and
explained her gift of being able to communicate with animals.

"Hold on a sec, you can talk to any animal in their own
language? And understand what they're saying to you? EVERY
single animal?" Eva asked.

"As far as I know, yeah. Even Ralph. But this is our secret.
You can't tell anyone about this, not even your mom, Eva! Or
your parents, Till!"

"I can't believe this," Till said. "I knew you were special, Lily
Bowers, but this is beyond incredible!"

"Just wait, this is nothing." As if Lily just gave the cue to raise the theater curtain, a bright light filled the sky. Mother Nature appeared and slowly descended from the treetops.

Even when she's sick with hardly any feathers, she's still beautiful.

Lily turned to her friends. "Meet Mother Nature. She's very ill and asked me to help save the animals and also save her. When animals are abused or killed, she becomes weak but usually has the strength to recover. But since there is more animal cruelty now than ever, she's unable to recover. If this continues, she won't be able to watch over us. She will die and if she dies, all that she takes care of will die with her. That means humans too. Life as we know it will cease to exist."

Mother Nature tried to speak, but only a faint whisper came out of her mouth.

Covering her mouth, Eva began to tear up. Till just stared.

"It's very upsetting. I cried too when I met Mother Nature and Alo. I first thought it was a dream when Alo visited me the night before school started, but then I realized it wasn't a dream after all."

"That night, I found out that I can speak to animals. But that's not all. I have been chosen to help save Mother Nature. If I save enough animals, I can help save her, but that's where I need help."

Pausing to take a deep breath, Lily looked at Alo for encouragement. He nodded with approval to continue.

"My new forest friends are helping me, but now, I need your help too. I think if we can win this school competition and present our idea to the government, maybe, just maybe, they will ban animal testing. It's not enough to have a ban in the cosmetic industry. We need it in the medical and scientific fields as well, so we need the government's help."

"I'll do anything to help," Till replied, and Eva nodded in agreement. She was still sobbing silently, unable to speak.

"I must go now," Mother Nature whispered. "Thank you, Eva and Till, for helping our beloved Lily. We have much faith in her, and now that I have met you, I feel confident she has the right teammates on her side. Lily, call on me if you need my help. You know I am always here for you."

She vanished into thin air, this time leaving a flurry of ascending white sprinkles where she had stood.

Eva looked up. "I can't believe she exists! We've all heard about Mother Nature, but wow, she really exists! And she's so beautiful!"

In a choked-up voice, she continued. "I can't believe we're killing her. This is worse than my parents getting a divorce. I feel like my whole world is collapsing on top of me." Lily hugged Eva, who then cried even more.

Till paced back and forth, rubbing his hands together. He scrunched up his face so much – Lily called it his 'thinking face' – that Lily was scared his brain cells were gonna pop out from the pressure.

"We have to win that competition! Let's get to work. Come with me!" Till grabbed Lily and Eva's hands and started toward home.

Then, he stopped suddenly, causing the two girls to lunge forward. He dropped their hands and returned to Alo, who was still sitting next to the flat rock, watching them in silence.

"Excuse me, Alo. I'm sorry, that was rude. Will you come with us?" Till asked.

Alo stood up, lifted his head for a sniff, then bowed at Till, turned around, and walked away in the other direction.

"Did I say something wrong?"

"Oh no, he said goodbye by sniffing you. He has to take care of Mother Nature now. That's his main job. He visits me at night sometimes though, and if we desperately need his help, all I have to do is howl. Let's go back to my house. We have a lot of work to do."

They walked back along the narrow path in silence.

Till abruptly stopped again, causing Eva to bump into him. "If you win this competition and go to Berlin, do you really think the government will ban animal testing for good? That just seems too optimistic."

"I don't know, but I have to try. Mother Nature has known me since I was born. They all have. I can't disappoint them. They're depending on me. Besides, I can't just sit here and watch her die, nor can I ignore what's happening to those poor, innocent lab animals."

"You're right, but how the heck is this going to work out?" Eva asked.

"I have no clue. I honestly don't know what I'm doing. Alo's been trying to get me to believe in myself and told me about a few children our age who have done some amazing things. So I know it's possible, but still, I'm scared I'll fail."

"Well, if it's any consolation, I believe in you!" Till said.

"I do too. We're in this together, and we'll make it work," Eva added.

"Thanks, that really means a lot!"

They walked into Lily's room. Ralph was on the floor with his head up, sniffing the air by her desk. Lily asked if he wanted her to put him on her desk. He did.

With excitement in her gait, Eva walked over and knelt down to look at him eye to eye. "Hi, Ralph, nice to finally really meet you!"

Ralph made some squeaky noises.

"He said he is honored to finally be able to communicate with you, his favorite human next to me. No offense, Till."

Till just nodded in acceptance.

Then, they talked about who was going to do what over the next few days.

Till's job was to create a video about what the future would look like if Mother Nature died. Eva was going to meet with her mom's friend who volunteered at the animal rights organization. Lily was going to research more about alternative methods to animal testing.

"I think we need a name for our group. What do you think?"

"What about 'Mother Nature's Little Helpers'?" Eva suggested.

"Or 'The Animal Activists of Reinhardswald' or 'The Reinhardswald Healers'?" Till asked.

They brainstormed for a few minutes.

"I got it: 'TAR: The Animal Rescuers'!" Lily said. "Plain, simple, and says it all!"

"Yeah, that's it!" Till and Eva both agreed.

Lily wrote it down on her notepad and stuck it to the corner of her computer. Not that she could ever forget that name, but she just wanted to see how it looked in writing. It looked and felt right! "The Animal Rescuers it is!"

18

WHAT DO WE HAVE HERE?

Lily didn't have school for the next two weeks. It was fall break, so there was plenty of time to work on the presentation and hang out with her best friends.

Even after they returned to school, they spent every free minute together.

Halloween was the only break they took. As planned, Till dressed up as a tornado, Eva as a mummy, and Lily as a deer zombie.

The entire house was decorated from top to bottom, as it was every year because Lily's parents always hosted a dinner party with their closest friends on Halloween.

When they finished trick-or-treating, Eva and Till came over to Lily's house to sleep over. It was a school night, but they promised their parents to be in bed by nine.

They brought some snacks up to Lily's room and started to play a board game.

"Boof! Skifsh!" Eva and Till quickly turned their heads to where the sudden sound came from and saw Alo's shadowy face gleaming at them outside from the balcony.

"Does he always do that?" Eva asked, shaking.

"Yes, but I'm used to it by now." Lily opened the door for Alo. As he crept inside, Lily noticed his tail was stuck between his legs.

"Are you okay? Is something wrong?" she asked.

"No, I am fine. I just should not roam in the woods tonight. One of our leaders and a very dear friend of mine was shot on All Hallow's Eve two years ago because, according to legend, a werewolf attacked the residents over a hundred years ago and the hunters made a pact to go out each year and make sure that never happens again.

"Every year since then, hunters roam the area, looking for us. They already blocked all entrances to the forest so no one enters during the witching hour. Have you seen the signs?"

Lily nodded.

"Maybe they are scared of wolves, who knows, but I thought the best hiding place would be in a house full of humans."

"Wow, I didn't know that about the hunters, but then again, I don't spend that much time in the woods on Halloween. I've never heard any shots though," Till said after Lily translated Alo's story.

"We are nowhere to be found on Halloween anymore. Or any day for that matter. We make sure we are invisible to humans. Good thing we can smell you from miles away."

As if that wasn't enough to frighten young preteen girls, Till started to tell his favorite scary story. For the next two hours, they told stories, laughed, and 'muah ha ha'd' underneath the tent made of sheets with a flashlight.

Then, the stairs creaked. "Ssshhh!" Lily quickly turned off the flashlight, hoping she could keep Alo unnoticed.

"Goodnight Lily, Eva, and Till. Time to go to bed now," Lily's mom said.

"Let us just finish this one story, and then we'll go to bed. I promise," Lily said, tightly holding the blanket over Alo just in case her mom tried to peek in to kiss her goodnight.

"Okay, but then no dilly-dallying after that, you hear?"

"Yes, Mom, thanks so much, good night!"

They quietly giggled for another hour or so, and once they were sleepy, Alo jumped over the balcony and sped into the woods.

It was now Wednesday afternoon, a week before Lily had to stand on stage. The Animal Rescuers, Lily, Eva, and Till, were waiting at the bus stop when Viktoria appeared out of nowhere.

She stood very close to Till, almost leaning on him, and with a flip of her beautiful long, wavy red hair, smiled and said, "I can't wait to see you on the basketball court this weekend." As Viktoria passed by, she turned and gave Lily an "I'm watching you!" glare.

"Bbrrrrr, it sure got cold," Lily said, not referring to the weather.

Till started playing basketball when he was six. Since he was taller than all the other boys, it was easy for him to make hoops. He even liked basketball better than soccer, which is uncommon in Germany.

And tomorrow was a big game with their school rival.

Ahhhhhh. Lily stopped thinking about basketball and finally realized why Viktoria looked so sad the other week when Till yelled at her. She liked Till. And from the way she had just acted, she liked him a LOT.

Till didn't seem to notice anything though.

Typical boy! SO oblivious!

Lily slightly shook her head but didn't want to even think about the two of them becoming a couple and holding hands, so she kept silent.

Eva noticed it too though and laughed, "Till, what the heck was THAT?"

"What do you mean? Oh, Viktoria? She can be really sweet when she wants to be."

"Um, no, Till, she was giving you The Look. I think she likes you!" Eva said.

"Nonsense, it doesn't mean anything. She's always like that." Till nervously rustled his books in his backpack.

"Maybe to you but not to anyone else. Wake up, boy."

"Leave him alone, Eva. Can't you see it's making him uncomfortable? Let's just go to my house and find out where we're at with this presentation. I'm starting to get nervous! Eeeeeeek, we only have one week left!"

They spent the rest of the afternoon comparing notes and fine-tuning their plans and creative ideas.

After dinner, Eva and Till went home. Lily printed her presentation so that they could stay after school and do research at the school library.

It rained heavily all night, and the next morning was no different. Lily put her presentation in a thick folder to protect it just in case her backpack got wet. As Till and Lily walked to the bus stop, Viktoria ran right in between them, pushing Lily off to the side, causing her to trip and fall to her knees.

Till started to call after her, but Lily stopped him. "It's okay, I'm alright. Just ignore her; no need to start a fight."

But he didn't want to give up. He was mad and didn't say a word the rest of the way to school. He just glared at Viktoria during the whole ride. At one point, she turned around and flashed him a big smile, which made him even redder with anger.

Finally, the lunch bell rang after a busy morning of politics, math and sports. Lily and Eva headed straight to the cafeteria to meet Till. While picking at their food, they went over Lily's presentation.

"What are you working on?" A shrill voice from behind Lily caused her to cringe with discomfort. It was Viktoria.

"None of your business!" Till shooed her away like a pesky young sibling.

"Who peed in your cornflakes this morning? Hope you show some of your spunk on the court on Saturday! Getting excited yet?" she asked.

"Viktoria, please, we have work to do!" Till's voice got louder.

"Fine, I'm going already. You don't have to yell at me, sheesh!" Viktoria flipped her hair, back straight and nose in the air, and walked off.

They were working so intently, they didn't hear the last bell and found they were the only ones left in the cafeteria.

"We're going to get kicked out soon. Let's go to the library now," Eva suggested and started to pack up their stuff.

After a few minutes, Lily jumped, "Uh oh, I think I left a part of my presentation in the cafeteria on the floor. I'll be right back." Lily fled out of the library.

In a slow jog, she reached the cafeteria only to stop dead in her tracks before opening the door. Through the glass, she saw Viktoria reading her presentation.

Storming in, Lily grabbed the stack of papers, looked underneath the table to make sure she had everything, and said, "These are mine, thank you very much!"

Of all days for her to have cafeteria duty.

Lily hurried back to the library, hoping Viktoria didn't get to read too much.

The meeting wrapped up with ideas for the film and a plan to shoot some more scenes in the woods. Till was jumping up and down in his seat and flailing his arms all over the place.

Lily had never seen him so excited about anything except basketball and soccer. *I wish I got that on video!*

Eva started talking about what she should ask her mom's friend.

"It would be helpful to know how to shop consciously. You know, what symbols to trust, how to read labels and what the ingredients mean?" Lily suggested.

Eva's face dropped. Lily scrunched her eyebrows together but then remembered how much Eva loved shopping and always bought the products with the prettiest packaging or the sweetest smells. The thought of having to boycott her favorite brands that weren't cruelty-free might be a bit upsetting for Eva.

"Oh, Eva, you'll be fine," Lily reassured her. "There are plenty of quality cruelty-free products out there, just wait and see. We can go shopping together, okay?"

"Pfft, girls," Till snickered.

19

THE ANIMAL RESCUERS AT WORK

They continued working for the rest of the afternoon until the last school bus came.

When she arrived home, Lily still had time to call CAAT-Europe, located at the University of Konstanz in Germany. She wanted to learn more about the methods that would hopefully replace animal testing very soon.

CAAT stood for the Center for Alternatives to Animal Testing. Lily had a fascinating conversation with the CEO and cofounder who explained NAMs, the abbreviation for New Approach Methodologies. He mentioned three methods: in silico, which use computer-modeling techniques, and HTS (high throughput screening) and in vitro, which use human cells from hair or skin.

Lily thanked him for his time and researched more about how these methods worked.

And now, she had all the information she needed and could concentrate on designing her presentation, the part she most looked forward to.

Lily loved to draw and was just learning how to create

graphics on the computer. She also knew if she needed help, she could ask Eva, who was even better at graphics.

The Animal Rescuers spent the following afternoon in the woods making videos. It was a breezy fall day and luckily not a rainy one.

The colored leaves had now formed a thick damp carpet on the forest ground, which was good because otherwise Lily would have been tempted to play in them. There was no time for fun though. It was time to work, and Till was on a rigid schedule.

He directed the set just like a natural born movie director.

Whenever he needed an actor, he asked Lily to call upon one - either a squirrel, or a wolf, or a group of deer - to play out the scene. He described the scenes to Lily, and she translated them to the animals.

Eva sat still on a rock and rubbed her hands on her arms. "I finally understand why you come to the forest so much, Lily!" she murmured. "I will remember this day forever!"

Lily nodded in Eva's direction with a smile and continued with her work. "Okay, birch tree on the left, please sway back and forth and after three seconds, crash your largest branch on your left down to the ground, and ... 3 ... 2 ... — 1." And the birch tree did exactly what Lily told him.

"Dear cute, little red squirrel on the second branch over there, please, scurry down to my feet, look up at me with big scared eyes as if you were starving to death, and then after I shake my head, walk away slowly with a look of despair and disappointment in your eyes. And whimper a bit too, please."

And bam, that's exactly what that cute, little red squirrel did.

This went on all afternoon. Eva sat quietly taking pictures and videos to show Lily and Till later.

"You two have no idea what you're missing," Eva blurted. "This is magical!"

At the end of the day, Lily called out to everyone to gather around in a circle.

She looked around, smiled, and said in Animalish, "I am so very proud of all of you. You did a wonderful job. Thank you for helping us. And thank you for making this the most incredible day of my life."

Tears started to form in the corners of her eyes. Her voice cracked. "I'm still not sure if we can help your friends, but we'll do our very best. In a few days, I hope to win this competition. If we are successful, we have a chance to make a real difference. We have the chance to save Mother Nature. Thank you once again! I'm truly grateful, and I love each and every one of you. We have to go now, but I'll be back."

"That was aMAzing!" Lily said, jumping up and down on their way home. She hadn't felt that exhilarated in a long time.

"And, Till, you rocked it out there!" And before she knew it, she gave him a big hug and kissed him on the lips!

Shocked, Till's stare and bulging eyes made Lily quickly tear herself away from him.

"Oh, I'm so sorry, I was just so excited! I don't know why I did that. I'm sorry," Lily said nervously.

Till just smiled and shrugged his shoulders, "It's okay, Lil, I kinda liked it," and started walking again.

Eva grabbed Lily by the arm and whispered, "What was that?"

"I don't know. It was nothing, absolutely nothing."

When they arrived at Lily's house, Till said, "I have to start editing this, so I'll see you tomorrow morning when I pick you up, alright?"

"Okay, have a good night and thanks again for all your help. You're a lifesaver."

"No, I'm just a good friend."

Eva left too. Her mom was home, and she wanted to spend some time with her.

Lily went up to her room and plopped down on her bed.

I can't believe I kissed Till! On the lips! What was I thinking?

But it was done, and there was no turning back time now. Not even worth thinking about it anymore really. They were best friends. And she was too young to be thinking about boys.

After dinner, her mom came up to her room to read a story together.

Her mom read three pages, then Lily read the next three pages, and it continued like that until the chapter was complete. Lily would have preferred to lie back, relax, and listen, but her mom said she wanted to feel like a child again and be read to, too.

That night, Lily dreamt of her friends in the forest with Mother Nature watching over them. She had full-feathered wings and felt healthy again. The animals were rejoicing and dancing around the trees. The forest animal babies were running, jumping, and playing around the river bank.

Without warning, the sun rays beaming down between the tree branches faded. The bright blue sky turned gray, almost black.

The animals scattered, and Lily was left alone, feeling the shivering cold, dark, wetness of the fall air. She looked down to her feet, but instead of seeing the forest ground full of leaves, she saw sand from the bottom of the ocean. In a panicked attempt, she tried to breathe, but nothing came in. And nothing came out as she tried to scream.

A surge of energy jolted her upright in bed. Sweat ran down her face; she heaved and struggled to draw breath into her lungs.

Exhausted, she dropped her dead weight onto her pillow. Tears streamed from her eyes, meeting the sweat and causing a raunchy, salty taste to cover her somewhat chapped lips.

She didn't understand how such a horrible nightmare could interrupt her sleep after such a magical day. Why was she panicking? Things were going so well.

Not wanting to think about it anymore, she closed her eyes and counted. One ... Two ... Three ... Four. That's all she was able to count before she fell back into a deep slumber.

Over the weekend, they finished up their presentation, and Lily practiced it in front of Eva and Till on Monday, then in front of her parents on Tuesday. She spent the rest of Tuesday evening fine-tuning the presentation and picking out her clothes.

And being nervous.

Lily had been on stage before when she played a cat and a maid in two plays in elementary school. Never before had she been on stage alone and had to speak in front of the whole school.

Over 700 classmates and teachers were going to be in that auditorium watching her.

Not being able to sleep well at all – also for fear of having another nightmare – she got up early the next morning, and her mom helped her with her hair and fixed her a hearty breakfast.

"How are you feeling, dear?" Lily's mom asked.

"Could be better. I didn't sleep well."

"Are you nervous? Just remember why you're doing this. Don't think about those people in the audience, think about the animals you're trying to save. You can do this. I know you can. You're well-prepared, and if you present it like you did last night, you have a really good chance of winning, I just know it! I'm SO excited for you. I wish I could be there with you, cheering you on."

Unfortunately, only the students and teachers were allowed to attend.

Lily finished her orange juice and went upstairs to get ready. Ralph gave her a few words of encouragement and reminded her to look at the coin again.

Why do I keep forgetting about this coin?

Shaking her head in disappointment, she picked it up. The circle of six hands appeared again, holding each other tight, but as she turned it over, the words dispersed and reformed to say: "Treat your worst enemy with respect."

What should that mean? I don't have any enemies.

Looking at her watch, she jumped. It was time to go! Scrambling to get her stuff ready, she quickly said bye to Ralph and practically tripped downstairs.

"You're as nervous as I am!" Lily noticed Till was just as clumsy.

"I just hope my video doesn't mess up," Till said.

"I'm sure it'll be just fine. Relax, you'll do great! I'm a complete wreck, let me tell you!"

"You'll do great, trust me. If anyone can pull this off, it's you! Come on, let's go, the school is waiting for you."

On their way to school, Lily looked up and saw that old woman with the black cloak across the street. The woman came over to greet Lily.

She took Lily's hand in her own hand and looked down at her. "I can feel that you have a big challenge ahead of you. Look at me." Lily looked up. "This challenge is nothing you can't handle. You are going to do well. That is all I know. I can feel your energy, and it is positive and pure. Good luck, Lily."

"How did you know my ... name?" But as soon as Lily said

'name,' the old woman was already on the other side of the street and hurried away.

"Who was that?" Till asked.

"A good friend, but I don't know her name," Lily said.

"Must not be that good of a friend if you don't know her name," Till jibed.

20

RESPECT YOUR ENEMIES

Lily watched the old lady until she couldn't see her anymore. When they got to the bus stop, they met an equally excited Eva, who wouldn't stop talking.

The bus was full of excited children. Lily's stomach turned more somersaults than ever before. As soon as they arrived at school, they walked straight to the auditorium and looked at the bulletin board outside the main door in the hallway.

Lily was number eight on the list. There was no title or description to what the students were presenting, only their names and presentation times.

Thinking back, for her application, Lily only had to submit a title and a short description and why she felt passionate about this subject. A total of forty-three applications were turned in, but only fifteen were approved. And each student had fifteen minutes to present their idea.

Lily also didn't know who else was going to be on stage that day. Apparently, no one in her class, otherwise she would have found out about that.

While inspecting the entire list more closely, her heart

suddenly jumped in her throat when she spotted one name: Viktoria Hein. Lily started to choke.

"Uh oh, guess she's presenting today, too? Ugh," Eva leaned in, sensing Lily's fear.

"Yeah, I just saw her name too, don't worry about her though. She can't do you any harm up there!" Till put his arm around Lily and held her tight for a second.

Still unable to talk, Lily just nodded.

She parted ways with her friends, who went to the sound and lighting area. Till was in charge of the video presentation, and Eva was going to work the lighting. They'd spent the past two afternoons learning and testing out their equipment.

"Ready to drown?" A shrill voice startled Lily from behind. It was Viktoria. "I see you're up after me. Good luck, you're gonna need it, clumsy!" A cool breeze going up Lily's body followed Viktoria's sinister laugh.

Viktoria then took the gum out of her mouth and smashed it right on Lily's name on the piece of paper on the bulletin board and walked off.

Feeling ill to her stomach, Lily stormed off backstage to get her mind off Viktoria and practice her script in peace and quiet.

The auditorium was jam-packed with students, who were relieved to be somewhere other than in class.

It was loud, and Lily couldn't concentrate, so she gave up trying.

If I don't know my script by now, I won't learn it in the next few hours either.

Instead, she closed her eyes to try to drown out the sounds of the crowd and the nervous pacing of the students getting ready for their presentations and daydreamed about being in the forest with Alo, the other animals, and Mother Nature.

And about kissing Till. Still unsure what THAT was all about.

The crowd clapped, causing her to jump. The competition was about to begin, and the first student went up on stage.

Lily paid close attention. The boy talked about all the plastic in the oceans killing birds and marine life. It was a pretty impressive presentation, and, like hers, a heartbreaking topic.

The next one was about the digital world and how teens should limit their time on their cell phones and spend more time with each other.

The third presenter showed images of how clothes were made. The children who worked endless hours in Asian factories and the amount of waste that was produced in the fashion and textile industry.

Wow, what is going on? Nothing seems to be right these days. What would aliens think of humans on Earth if they suddenly came down today and saw these problems we've created?

A deep sadness embodied Lily, forcing her to sit down. Her hands swiped her eyes before tears started to form.

I can't get upset now. I have to be strong.

She daydreamed about life on Earth without any harm being done to humans, animals, or our environment. That was the world she wanted to live in.

Feeling more at peace, she watched the next three presentations and felt the inner beauty of these students trying to do something good in the world. Their pain felt familiar, and she wondered if they, too, had help from Mother Nature.

Her positive thoughts were abruptly interrupted when Viktoria bumped into her while walking toward the stage. "Oh, did I just bump into you? I'm SO sorry, but I need to get on stage to show you who's boss!" Viktoria raised her left brow and walked on stage.

Lily couldn't move. She watched intently as Viktoria started her presentation.

A feeling of disgust and rage quickly overcame her body.

Viktoria's presentation was about testing on animals for medical research, but she wasn't talking about helping the animals. Instead, she talked about helping humans. She made it sound like animal testing was a positive, necessary process.

She explained how so many human lives were saved because tests were done on animals. For example, that insulin therapy was only possible because animal researchers killed dogs to remove and test their pancreas' in the 1920s.

Lily put that in her presentation as well, but Viktoria left out the most important part: the essential clues that the scientists received on insulin treatment actually came from observing human patients, not from the canine experiments.

Viktoria then mentioned how researching the brain of a monkey helped Parkinson's patients.

That, too, was a twisted truth. Surgeons identified the best place to put electrodes into Parkinson's patients' brains to help improve their symptoms decades before performing brain surgery and useless tests on monkeys.

Viktoria even talked about effectively using mice and rats to detect lung cancer by filling their lungs with smoke.

Okay, that's it, this is just plain ridiculous! Didn't she read that smoking doesn't cause cancer in mice and rats? The scientists found out that smoking causes cancer after performing studies on humans!

Lily was outraged. How dare she steal her idea and turn it upside down like that?

Lily's phone beeped. It was a text from Till. "Grrrr. Don't worry. You got this! You're presenting the truth! Just be yourself, stay strong & remember why you're doing this! xoxo."

Viktoria was finally finished with her skewed facts. She bowed and slowly walked off stage during her applause.

Lily was relieved when she walked off to the opposite end of the stage because she had no desire to face her right now.

Two more and then I'm up! She had to get ready, so she

slipped in an empty dressing room and texted Marc, who agreed to assist her.

"And now, we present to you Lily Bowers. We're excited to find out what you're passionate about and how you plan to make changes," Mr. Donau, an eighth-grade science teacher, announced and walked off stage before Lily had the chance to walk on.

Lily breathed in deeply and waited for her signal.

Click! The stage lights were turned off, and the entire auditorium was black.

Till started the sound effects. A low growl rumbled out of the loudspeakers and slowly transformed into a loud collage of screeches, squeaks, barks, hisses, and squawks.

Images of scared animals banging on the bars of small cages were projected onto the huge screen. Slowly, one by one and then faster and faster until the last image appeared and stayed.

It was of a monkey in a cage. With blood running down his face, piercing eyes staring in the distance and a thick metal bolt coming out of the top of his head. The video faded and with a loud click, a spotlight shone on Lily.

She was sitting cramped up in a cage, dressed in a tight brown turtleneck long-sleeved shirt and black jeans and brown gloves. Blood (fake of course) was running down her face, eyes wide open, and her dirty hands tightly held the bars. A handmade bolt attached to the top of her head. Projecting her monkey scream as loud as she could, she shook the cage uncontrollably.

The audience went silent.

"This ... is the life of hundreds of thousands of animals. Innocent animals living in small cages. Fear, excruciating pain, and loneliness are all they know."

"And for what? To make us prettier. To pump us up with medication and to clean up what we make dirty."

Lily then talked about several medical breakthroughs. The same ones Viktoria mentioned.

No matter how much she wanted to highlight the fact that Viktoria wasn't telling the entire truth, she remembered what the coin read: "Respect your enemies."

With more confidence than she had ever had, she presented the way she practiced and left Viktoria out of it completely, just like a professional.

She used facts and figures to support her case that animal testing was inefficient, making it dangerous in the medical field, and introduced the three New Approach Methodologies (NAMs): in silico, HTS (high throughput screening) and in vitro.

She added everything that was relevant, but also made sure she kept it interesting and entertaining.

"If we continue harming and killing animals, this is what our beautiful Earth will look like in a few decades."

The stage faded to black, and the next video started.

The crowd gasped as they saw death overcome the forest. Squirrels, mice, deer, owls, and other birds were lying everywhere. No blood, just still bodies covered in the thick carpet of leaves on the ground.

The tree branches drooped down. One tree lifted a branch in desperation, but slammed it back down, too weak to carry its own weight.

The next scene showed Lily walking carefully through the forest, tears in her eyes. Stopping as soon as she arrived at the graveyard of dead animals covering the forest floor, she cried even harder.

A cute, little red squirrel walked to her feet and peered up at her with a frightened and hungry look in his eyes. Lily knelt down and shook her head. She had nothing to feed the poor squirrel. Disappointed, the squirrel slowly walked off in desperation.

The next scene was in another part of the forest. Ten wolves were sitting in a circle, howling at the full moon above. They were hovering over something in the center of the circle.

The video zoomed in closer and closer to show what was in the center but suddenly stopped at the wall of wolves. Through the cracks between their bodies, a shiny white object flickered but was unidentifiable.

Fade to black.

The spotlight went back on Lily, still locked up in the cage.

21

STANDING OVATION

"If we continue to harm and kill animals in unnecessary experiments, we will kill the most important being on Earth. Mother Nature. The one who looks over all living creatures, in the forest, underneath the dirt, in the sea, on mountaintops, and in caves. Every living being will die without her protection. Even us, humans."

"We have to start making changes today if we want our children to grow up in a healthy world."

"A wise man once said, 'The greatness of a nation and its moral progress can be judged by the way its animals are treated.' That wise man was Mahatma Gandhi.

"Let's live in his example and be a great nation. One that cares for its animals.

"Another wise soul reminded me that if we respect Mother Nature and all she takes care of, we will be at peace with ourselves. If we're at peace with ourselves, we're at peace with others. And if we're all at peace with others, we will have world peace.

"It's all about respecting all animals, human included. Yes, I believe in fairy dust. Absolutely," Lily giggled.

"But I also believe in the power of people. We can make a change. No matter how young we are. We have a voice. And we have a choice. We can start by not harming animals for useless experiments."

"Do you know why animals are still being tested on?" Lily pointed to a few kids in the front row who shook their heads and shrugged. "I didn't until recently either."

"Why are these newer methods not standard practice if they're cheaper, more accurate, and humane? Because of tradition. Because humans are scared of change. They're used to doing something a certain way and have a hard time adapting to new ways, even if they're better. Even if they make more sense! Why change a well-running system, right?

"Well, that running system is destructive and cruel, that's why you have to change it. Because change, my dear friends and teachers, will keep our world turning. It's what will keep us alive and well!

"There are things you can start doing today. Easy things. You can support ethical companies that don't test on animals and not buy from those that do.

"But that's not all. You can learn more about animal testing and the New Approach Methodologies. Here are a few:

1. If you're interested in the medical research field, you can think about a career in a laboratory that uses NAMs and become an advocate for humane methods.
2. Call and write your city government officials to take a stand on banning animal testing.
3. Donate to or volunteer at an animal rights organization.
4. Spread awareness on social media.
5. Organize or participate in a protest and/or a petition.

"If you need any other suggestions, just ask me.

"There are many simple things you can do to help save animals from testing. You can start making a change today!" Lily's voice got louder with each word.

"I ask all of you today. Do you want change?"

Only a few weak voices murmured.

Lily asked again, "I can't hear you. Do you want change?"

The crowd yelled, "YES!"

"I still can't hear you, do you want change?" Lily screamed at the top of her lungs.

"YEEEESSSSS!" the audience screamed after her.

"Do you want to save animals?" she yelled back into the crowd.

"YEEEESSSSS!" the audience shouted back.

"Well, then please send me to Berlin to talk to those who have the power to ban animal testing for good!"

"But first, GET ME OUT OF HERE!" Lily rattled the cage and ferociously screeched like a monkey.

The audience sprung from their seats and wildly applauded.

Marc jumped up on stage to help Lily. She crawled out, looked out into the crowd, smiled, and modestly whispered, "thank you," as she took a bow.

Her body vibrated from the thunderous applause.

"You were amazing. That was the best presentation so far! Congratulations," Marc whispered as he helped carry the cage offstage.

"Thank you so much!" Lily beamed a bright red.

"Squeeeeeeee. How was it?" Lily asked Eva and Till as they ran toward her.

"Incredible, you took all the other presentations to another level!" Till hugged her.

"I'm so happy for you, Lily. You rocked it out there!" Eva went in for a hug, too.

"I'm hungry, let's eat!" Till said after they announced the lunch break.

Too excited to eat, Lily just sat there and stared at her salad.

Eva was talking non-stop about Lily's presentation until Till motioned for her to calm down. "You look a little pale. Would you like to get some air?" Till asked, nodding toward Lily. She nodded. They spent the rest of their break outside sitting on the bench in silence.

The rest of the presentations were good, too. There were two others that also received a standing ovation. Lily had a tough field of competition!

Her stomach turned a few more times that afternoon.

There was a short recess for the ten-member jury to consult with each other and choose a winner. The final bell rang, and the students and teachers scuffled back into their seats.

Lily took Eva and Till's hands and stood between them backstage with the other contestants.

Whatever happens, I'll be okay with it.

The spotlight came back on, and Mr. Donau got up on stage.

He called all the presenters to the stage.

"Good luck!" Eva and Till said in unison.

Lily went up on stage, making sure she stood as far away from Viktoria as possible.

"This was the first time we've organized such an event," Mr. Donau said. "But I don't believe it'll be the last. We've learned so much in the past few hours about how we can help the environment, save our planet, save animals, and even ourselves. I would like to thank all fifteen ambitious young adults who presented on stage today. You are our future. You have the power to change the world, and I encourage all of you and those who were not on stage today to follow through with your plans and ideas. The entire school administration encourages you to find and follow your passion!"

"BUT, unfortunately, we can only send one of you to Berlin. The jury has picked the winner. Ms. Funkel, please bring me the envelope."

The butterflies in Lily's stomach were now riding on roller coasters.

Carefully opening the sealed envelope, Mr. Donau read the name on the piece of paper and paused. He looked at each of the students on stage, turned to the audience, and continued.

"Girls and boys, fellow teachers and mentors, I'm proud to announce the first winner of the 'Find Your Passion' competition. This lucky person will be awarded a free five-day trip to Berlin in a comfortable four-star hotel, a trip to the museum of his or her choice, a date with the German parliament to present his or her idea, AND an adequate daily allowance for food and souvenirs. Not just for the winner, but also for three other family members or friends."

"And now, without further ado, the winner is--" Lily closed her eyes.

"Lily Bowers, for her brilliant presentation, 'The Truth about Animal Testing and Alternatives to Live By.'"

The audience cheered and applauded. Lily's body froze solid.

The girl next to her nudged, "Pssst, Lily, you won. Congratulations! Go, get your trophy."

Lily opened her eyes and hurried over to receive her trophy.

Her eyes fixated on the small, silver cup with the engraving: "Find Your Passion 2018: You Will Move Mountains."

Hmmm, that's what the lab director told me. And that ant!

Lily thanked Mr. Donau, who handed her the microphone.

She gasped. *Oh NO! I never prepared a winner's speech!*

She thanked Eva, Till, Marc, and her parents for their help and went on to say that she would do her best in Berlin and would continue her wish to save as many animals as possible. Then, she paused to thank her special friends, who know who they were, but were not in the audience. The speech ended with a promise to publish a list of simple things everyone can do to support the ban on animal testing.

The rest of the day was a complete blur to Lily. Everyone else who entered the contest congratulated her, except Viktoria.

Till told Lily later that he saw Viktoria slink offstage right after Mr. Donau announced her as the winner.

Lily's mom was waiting outside the school building to take her, Eva, and Till out to celebrate.

They had ice cream downtown and dinner at Lily's favorite place to eat, the Restaurant im Dornröschenschloss Sababurg (Sleeping Beauty's Castle). Once she was home, Lily went upstairs and told Ralph the entire story.

He was so excited that his head kept drooping from stretching it out so far.

Alo appeared at her window right as Lily turned off the light to go to sleep. She was happy to see him but fell asleep just as she started telling him about her day.

Falling asleep that night took less than ten seconds. Not that she counted, but Ralph did.

The next day at school was unlike any other. The smiles and congratulations while walking through the hallway were nice at first, but after a while, the attention became a bit annoying. And Lily wasn't too keen on constantly being stared at either.

I hope this settles down soon.

But she certainly didn't mind hearing praise from her friends.

"My mom has been buying cruelty-free stuff for years now. She is SO proud of you and wants to invite you to dinner, so let me know when you can come, okay?" Marc said on their way outside during recess.

"Oh, now you're hanging around a new boy, you sure do get around, Miss Flirty," Viktoria interrupted.

Lily stood up tall, looked Viktoria straight in the eye, and calmly said, "I only hang out with incredible people like him because not only is he intelligent and super creative, he has the amazing ability to make everyone around him laugh. Those are wonderful traits, and for that, I truly admire him.

"Come on, Marc, let's go outside where the sun is shining. It's too gloomy and depressing here." Lily gently took his hand and escorted him outside with her.

"Wow, that was really sweet of you to say, thanks."

"I meant every word," Lily said with a smile.

22

THINKING OF OTHERS

During lunch, Till looked very upset and didn't say much at all. "What's wrong?" Lily asked.

"I got my first 4 ever. On my last math test. I don't know if it's just because I spent all my time on the presentation or if this is going to be the year that's gonna slam me."

"At least a 4 is passing! I got a 6 on my English test last week!" Eva whined.

"Oh no. I'm so sorry. I didn't know!" Lily sighed. "I don't want either of you to get bad grades because of me. Did you talk to your teachers?"

"Yeah, but she was right. I just blew it this time," Till said.

"And you know I suck at English, Lily. It was just a matter of time," Eva said, putting her head down.

"I feel horrible. Eva, I can help you with English. We'll study together for the next test, okay? Till, I'm afraid I can't help you though. I'm really sorry. Is there anything else I can do?"

"You can't do anything, Lily. It's not your fault, but if I don't improve my grade in math, I won't qualify for the next robotics competition in January, and I was really looking forward to that. But maybe the next test won't be so bad. I don't know."

"I'm really sorry." Lily couldn't help but feel guilty.

"It's okay, what are ya gonna do?" Till replied. "I gotta go and study, see you two later."

Lily only had two weeks to prepare for the Berlin trip, but, already feeling guilty about their low grades, she didn't want to ask Till or Eva for any more help.

What did make her feel better though was that she was allowed to take three people with her, and since her dad chose to stay home and work, she invited them to come with her and her mom.

"They deserve it more than I do anyway," Lily's dad said.

Lily didn't want to put on a show in Berlin like she did on stage at school. She knew that politicians wanted facts and figures, not a show. Her mom helped her with the research and her dad with her presentation style.

Two days before the trip, Lily picked up the coin on her desk. It began to change right before her eyes and transformed into the old lady with the black cloak. On the other side, it read: "You have an incredible gift, use it wisely."

Lily called Alo. After only two minutes, he was on her balcony. "Wow, that was quick!" Lily let him in.

"I expected your call."

Lily showed him the coin.

"Yes, I knew it would change soon."

"Who's that old lady in the black cloak? I've seen her a few times. She must live near my house. She knows my name, but I don't know hers."

"She does not have a name. It would be demeaning to give her a human name that others share. She is more than that. She protects and cares for all living organisms. Lily, you know her well."

"What? How could that be? She's just an old woman I met at the bus stop!"

"Our beloved Mother Nature takes on many forms and plays any role needed at any particular time. She knew how much you loved and miss your great-grandmother and ... how to touch your heart. That was no coincidence you met her at the bus stop. That was her magic working."

"Once, I saw her transform into a life vest to save a drowning child in a lake. She chooses her appearances and whom she helps very carefully though, so if you have actually seen her, there is usually a good reason."

"But I can tell you're not gonna tell me what that reason is, huh?"

"I would if I could."

"Whatever. So, what does the coin mean?" Lily was getting a little annoyed. "I know I have this gift of communicating with animals and yes, it is incredible, but how can I use it wisely? I'm talking to you. I've spoken with my team in the forest. Aren't I using my gift wisely already?"

"Yes, you are. Sometimes, though, you have to stop looking at the obvious and start looking around you. You now have to convince others who are very set in their ways. What will it take to convince them?"

Alo turned around and looked at the door. "If I were to walk downstairs and into your living room, what would your parents do?"

"My dad would probably try to hit you with the TV. My mom would probably just faint," Lily said with an eye roll.

"Yes, because they view me as a threat to their existence. They would fear their own lives and try to protect yours. But, if a deer came walking into your living room, what would they do?"

"Hhmmm, I bet they would open the back door and lead her out, so she could go back into the woods."

"Correct. Every animal species has a natural way of igniting a particular emotion in humans. If you want humans to react a certain way, think of the animal that will create that particular reaction. And think of your audience. How do you want them to feel during your presentation?"

Lily spent a few minutes thinking about this question and finally blurted out, "I want my audience to feel sympathy for the lab animals."

"Ah, very good. And, which animals can help you with that?" Alo asked.

"I have no clue, just tell me," Lily replied with impatience. Alo frowned at her.

"Okay, okay, I'll figure it out myself," Lily sighed.

"Let me leave you with this one last thought: Listen to Mother Nature's message. She said 'USE' your talent wisely. Use US, Lily. We will do anything to help you. You do not have to do this alone."

Lily wasn't satisfied though. She wasn't alone. Her mom, Eva, and Till were going with her. But she didn't have time for this guessing game either. The trip to Berlin was in two days, and she was already finished with the preparation. Why didn't he just tell her what to do?

Lily turned to Ralph to complain.

"But Lily, Alo is your guide, not your drill sergeant. It is not his job to give you orders. His job is to help you become aware of a certain situation and your options. Your job is to listen and choose the right path."

"I know, but I'm already finished, what more do I need?" Lily worried that her presentation wasn't good enough.

"Apparently, a little help from your animal friends!" Ralph said. "The answer will come to you. Be patient and worry not."

"Thanks, but I AM worried. What if I never find the answer?"

"Then it was not meant to be. You will do fine. Relax. And eat some dinner. Your mom is going to call any second now."

"Lily, time for dinner," Lily's mom called from the bottom of the stairs.

"See, I can always smell when dinner is on the table! Enjoy, and save me some!"

Lily tossed and turned after going to bed.

Ralph started to hum, probably to try to calm her nerves.

"Thanks, Ralph," Lily whispered and at some point, she fell asleep.

Lily was suddenly in the middle of the dark, wet forest. She didn't recognize any trees or clearings.

Feeling a chill run through her body, she walked along a path and looked all around to try to see something familiar, but there was nothing.

A loud crack came from behind her. Turning around slowly, Lily had an eerie feeling enter her gut.

There stood a familiar creature. "I am going to get you, so you better start running!"

Lily shrieked, immediately turned back around, and started to sprint as fast as she could.

"I can smell your fear!" he shouted after her.

Lily took a deep breath.

Oh wow, I can smell my own fear, too. Maybe it's just my own sweat, but humans can't smell fear. We can maybe sense it, but we can't smell it. Or can we?

She stumbled over a log and turned around only to see him gaining on her.

There was a bigger log coming up. *I'm going to jump over it just like he did.*

She sprang herself up in the sky, and her left foot caught a small branch that caused her to fall hard on the ground.

"Owwwwww!" Lily grabbed her left leg and rolled over on her back.

She couldn't get away now. As soon as he caught up with her, he pinned her down and smiled.

Lily peered through the slits of her almost-closed eyes.

Drool started to drip from the corner of his mouth as he opened it wide, baring all his teeth.

"Gotcha!"

"Are you going to eat me?" she asked.

"I don't know about you, but I don't eat humans when I play 'Catch me if you can'—do you?"

Laughing, the wolf nudged Lily's cheek with his wet nose, "Wake up, wake up, Lily. It's time to go outside now!"

Lily gasped and awakened to find herself curled up in her warm bed.

Realizing it was yet another odd dream, she sighed and slowly got out of bed and got ready for school.

Lily walked out the front door to catch the bus with her head hanging low. She looked toward the bus stop to see if Till was waiting there. He wasn't there yet, but she also wasn't alone.

All over her front lawn were small animals! Puppies, kittens, bunnies, and doves. There must have been thirty or forty of them! She saw Sam, the owl on her team, sitting on a branch of the small tree.

Lily glanced around to see if anyone else was witnessing this. But thankfully, she was alone with them, so she asked quietly, "What are all of you doing here? Aren't you supposed to be home with your mommies?"

Sam flew down to the balcony rail. "I will make sure they all find their way back home. What's more important is your trip to Berlin. We want to help you with your presentation."

"But how? My presentation is already finished." Lily turned
to Sam, staring at her with his huge round eyes that didn't seem
to ever close shut.

Immediately, Lily felt calm again.

"What's going on here at the Bowers Zoo?" Till interrupted.

"They want to help me in Berlin, and you know what? I
think I finally know how! Come, let's go and I'll tell you on the
way to school."

She turned to Sam, "Thanks, you're a lifesaver! Thanks to
all of you! I have to go now, but you'll hear from me later this
afternoon. Have a wonderful day!"

Lily ran to Till as they hurried to the bus stop.

"Um, Lily, there were puppies and kittens all over your
lawn. I can understand Sam being there, or the doves, or
MAYbe even one deer, but where did the puppies and kittens
come from?"

"I guess from around town. I have no clue. They were just
on the lawn when I walked out."

Upon meeting Eva, Lily told them her new plan.

23

THE BEST PARTY IN PARLIAMENT

The taxi came to take them to the train station. Happy to find out they had a first-class cabin all to themselves, Till quickly took a window seat and laid his head on the side to fall back asleep.

"Didn't go to bed early enough, huh?" Lily, sitting across from him, gave him a gentle kick.

"I couldn't sleep well. I kept waking up because of all the howling, hooting, croaking, and chirping outside. It sounded like an animal choir's rendition of 'This is Not a Silent Night.' Didn't you hear them too?"

"I sure did, but the sounds actually helped me relax and fall asleep," Lily said with a smile.

As soon as they were out of the city, Lily's mom looked out the window. "Wow! Look at all those bunnies. There must be hundreds of them!"

Every single bunny was facing the train and standing upright on their back feet.

"They're standing at attention!" Eva nudged Till to wake up.

Lily winked at Eva and Till and spread her hand out flat on the window.

The train was moving pretty fast, but the line of bunnies seemed endless. Finally, after about five minutes, there were no more to be seen.

For the next two hours, they noticed the same thing happen with other animals. Deer bowed their heads as the train passed. Hundreds of different bird species flew alongside the train throughout the entire trip.

"Look at all those cute mice," Lily squeaked with joy.

Large groups of cats, dogs, and farm animals gathered too. Only the train stop areas were animal-free.

"Hello! This is your train conductor. If you haven't noticed already, look to your left now. We have a few hundred fans who want to wish us a safe journey."

Till joked, "If only he knew."

Lily's mom gave Till a funny look. "Knew what?"

"Err, um, that Lily's going to save them," Eva answered after a short, awkward silence.

They arrived at their train stop and walked a few blocks to their hotel.

Eva cooed while walking through the front entrance of the hotel. She stared at the modern paintings on the walls of the beautifully decorated lobby.

Lily and her mom went to the front desk to check in. They all had to share a room. But not just any room. It was a big suite with two bedrooms, one large bathroom with two sinks, and a living area with a couch and two large reclining chairs.

They enjoyed the rest of the afternoon roaming Berlin and stopped for dinner at a small, entertaining Italian pizzeria. Till laughed at every joke the pizza pie maker told while flipping the dough into the air.

Lily loved watching pizza bakers perform. She hardly ever saw dough flipping in Germany though, but faintly remembered a visit to New York where they watched pie flippers through the windows of Little Italy.

Best pizza in the world. That's what her dad always said anyway, but she didn't remember the taste of it.

Lily and her parents used to travel to New York twice a year to visit her grandparents before they moved to Germany. She really missed them and her old friends in Colorado. That was the hardest part about being an expat.

Every Christmas she wished for someone to invent a tele-portation "Beam me up" technology, but never got her wish granted. "There are only a few million brilliant engineers in Germany and in the States, why can't just one of them figure this out? Sheesh!" she often joked.

They enjoyed the busyness of a big city and walked the streets until it was late. Tomorrow was going to be a relaxing day since they had plans to visit a museum.

The next morning, they woke up and ate a hearty breakfast from the huge buffet in the hotel restaurant.

"Let's walk to the museum. It's not too far, and it's a gorgeous day," Lily's mom said.

Feeling like she could get away with anything, Lily really enjoyed roaming museums. Just like her dad, she was able to retain historical information. Her mom? Not so much.

"How can you remember all this stuff?" Lily's mom asked, giving up on reading every piece of information.

The last stop at the museum was the taxidermy exhibit. "Yay, finally, something really cool." Lily's mom eagerly scurried in.

A few steps in, Lily felt a surge to the left and almost stumbled over her two feet. As she started to walk straight again to follow her mother, the surge repeated, only this time, it tripped her up, causing her to fall on the ground.

"Oh, wow, are you OK?" Till held out his hand and without any effort, lifted her back up.

"Yeah, just can't seem to walk straight," Lily nervously smiled.

Literally being drawn into the room to the left, Lily surrendered, heart beating faster than a diving falcon.

There he was. In a glass box with the light shining on him. Looking all smug. And dead.

Lily looked deep into the eyes of a stuffed brown bear. Lily read the story of how this brown bear was an orphan who was raised by humans because his mother abandoned him. He then died prematurely because of a brain tumor.

"All I wanted was to be loved," a young voice whispered.

Lily looked around. She was alone in the room. Alone, with this bear who was stuffed.

"Is that you, bear?"

"I am his spirit. That's all we want. To be loved and free. Thank you, Lily, for being here and visiting me. I am honored."

"I'm so sorry for your pain and loss. Your soul lives on. Are you now at peace?"

"Yes. I am at peace. I am free and I am loved. But I worry for my relatives headed for extinction. I visit them during their darkest and loneliest hours to give them strength to carry on. It helps. Enough about me. I drew you near me because I wanted to say that I am proud of you. We all are here at the museum. We send you much luck. You are very loved."

"Hey, Lily, come over here, you have to see this," Lily's mom interrupted in a loud whisper.

Lily turned back to the bear, "Thank you for your kind words. I hope I can save your relatives someday."

Next, they took a boat ride along the Spree River and ate dinner while watching the setting sun at a local café. It was the perfect end to a fun day. At 8:00 pm, they were all back in their suite and went to bed early. Tomorrow was Friday, the day of Lily's presentation at the Parliament.

Lily was luckily able to fall asleep quickly and didn't wake up until her mom rubbed her head the following morning.

They had plenty of time to get ready and enjoyed another hearty breakfast. Lily didn't eat much though. Her stomach was twisting and turning. She managed to eat some muesli but compared to yesterday's breakfast, that was nothing.

After getting ready, Lily inspected herself in the mirror in her stylish pantsuit. She looked like a young business professional.

You can do this, Lily! She repeated that a few times out loud in a quiet voice.

Unfortunately, that little pep talk didn't help her nervous mind.

"Let me help you, dear," her mom offered after seeing Lily fidget with the zipper on her bag.

"Just remember, this won't be any different than your presentation at school. In fact, there's even less pressure now because you won't know anyone. But I bet, as soon as you walk out of there, they won't forget your name!"

"Your mom is right!" Till butted in. "All they'll be thinking about is how inspiring that Lily Bowers girl is and ask themselves what changes they can make!"

"Thanks, I really appreciate it," Lily said unconvincingly. "Okay, let's go. I'm ready!"

They walked the few blocks to the German Parliament and went through the security check. They were greeted by a friendly staff member who took them through a long hallway and into a waiting room.

Lily looked out the big window and saw a bunch of people walking around on the nicely kept grounds outside. It was a cool, sunny autumn day.

She went over her speech in her head until a man walked in to escort them into the room where all the politicians discussed their positions.

This is it. Keep calm and just do your best.

Lily's mom, Eva, and Till gave her a big hug, a few final words of encouragement, and followed closely behind. Lily was on her own this time. There was no big show, no bars to hide behind or spotlight. It was just her, a few slides, and her speech.

As soon as she walked in, the room became silent and all eyes fell on her. Everyone stood up and applauded as Lily walked to the podium. She apparently didn't need an introduction. They already awaited her and knew the reason why she was there.

She explained why she became passionate about animal rights, specifically about animal testing. She told them what she'd done over the past few months to change things in her own household with the help of her parents and how she planned to inspire others to do the same.

She kindly asked the man who escorted her in to dim the lights and start the film. And once again, the audience was brought into Lily's forest. Although this audience knew many of her facts and figures already, their reactions still seemed to be appalled and disgusted, which Lily didn't expect but was grateful to see.

Following the film, the lights came on, and Lily talked in-depth about the New Approach Methodologies and how they were safer, more effective, and cheaper.

She asked a politician in the front row why these methods weren't standard. He shrugged his shoulders.

"Do you know?" she asked a woman in the third row to the left. Silence.

"I'll tell you what I think. It's our mentality. That's all. It's not that it's expensive or time-consuming to make these changes. These changes are easy to make. But, we, as a human animal, are afraid of change. We sometimes don't want to adapt to new situations and surroundings. Instead of adapting, we continue doing what we've always been doing. Why change a running system, right? But doing the same inhumane acts out of tradition will not help us grow as a community."

She then asked everyone to stand up and walk over to the windows behind them where people were walking on the grounds.

The room became loud with the scuffling of hurried feet and whispers. Those whispers became louder as the politicians looked outside. Sounds of shock and a few loud bursts of outrage filled the air.

Thousands of puppies, kittens, deer, mice, doves, and owls were frolicking amongst the people. The adults were either frozen in dismay or busy taking selfies with their phones and the children were laughing and jumping with glee.

And then, as Sam predicted, Lily started to hear the laughter and cooing from the politicians. One by one, their shock transformed into what it seemed to be, love and sympathy.

A woman shrieked as a huge owl flew into the building through an open window and landed on the podium where Lily still stood. It was Sam. Lily winked at him.

In a loud voice, Lily called them back to their seats.

"Meet my friends who have gathered here today to help save their friends in cages. And meet Sam, my trusty companion, who helped me build up the courage to speak to all of you today."

Lily looked up at her mom, whose mouth hit the floor. She motioned to her mom, "And meet my mom, who also had no idea I had so many friends." Laughter filled the room.

"A few months ago, I was just as surprised as you are now. I also knew nothing about animal testing. I bought things from the store without thinking about how they were made, and I never questioned anything. But now that I know the damage I was doing, not only to innocent animals but also to our planet and ultimately to myself, I decided to inform myself and get some help from a few friends so that I could find the courage to come here and talk to you. You have the power to change things and stop the cruelty."

"Let's work toward a ban on animal testing today. I'm here to help get it done."

24

SPEAKER FOR THE ANIMALS

With those words, Lily left the podium and sat in the first empty seat she saw. The woman next to her stood up and started clapping. Everyone else followed suit. "Lily, stand up," the woman next to her nudged.

Sam circled the room three times before flying out the same window he entered.

Lily was escorted back to the podium by the German chancellor. "Lily, you are an impressive young girl, and I would feel honored to have you on our team!

"Personally, I would love to ban animal testing today, but it's not that easy. This will take a lot of time for us to make sure the alternative methods are better for everyone involved. We have to seek out experts in various fields, listen to all sides, and make the best decision based on all the information we have. And we may even have to support public companies and private institutions financially to make this change.

"That said, you are right. Enough is enough, especially if the alternative methods prove to be more accurate and cost-effective. We just have to take the proper steps to establish rules and guidelines, and this can't be done today.

"I'd like to propose setting up a committee to start working on a possible ban. Maybe you can help us with that because we need experts from various fields, and you certainly seem like the expert who is most qualified to speak for the animals."

Lily beamed with pride and smiled, showing off her deep dimples as she nodded.

"I'll assign you a partner who will be responsible for communicating with you throughout this process. But please, be patient. Rome wasn't built in a day, and this is just one issue we have to deal with. This will take time. Thank you for speaking with us today. You were not only convincing, you were also inspiring and for that, I thank you. Do you all agree?" Everyone in the room clapped again.

"Are you willing to be our official 'Speaker for the Animals,' Lily?"

"I would be honored to, thank you. Thank you with all my heart," Lily said as she accepted the Chancellor's hand and shook it confidently.

Till and Eva sprang up from their seats and ran to Lily.

"I knew you could do it. Congratulations," Till said and hugged her tightly.

"You were amazing. I'm so proud of you," Eva ripped Lily away from Till's hold.

Lily's mom wasn't too far behind and rushed up to her daughter. Stroking her hair, she said, "I knew you would do incredible things the minute I felt your first kick in my belly. I love you so much, dear."

The same man who escorted Lily, her mom, and friends, came up to lead them all out.

"One moment, please." Lily quickly ran to the window and opened it. The animals stopped frolicking and turned to look at her. With a huge smile, she breathed in as deeply as she could and let it out slowly. A fresh breeze blew over the lawn, and the animals jumped up and down in ecstatic celebration.

Mother Nature appeared as the old lady in the black cloak among the crowd of animals and took a few steps toward the building. She pulled off her hood, looked at Lily, smiled, and bowed. The animals bowed with her. Mother Nature nodded and gestured for Lily to return to the others and then turned around and disappeared into the crowd of animals. One by one, the animals dispersed, and the lawn was full of people again.

Lily turned back around to meet the others waiting at the door. It was time to celebrate!

When they arrived home, Lily's dad was waiting for them on the front porch. His warm welcome was very calming after such a whirlwind week.

"I'm so proud of you, sweetheart. You've made a real difference! Come on in."

"Surprise!" Lily jumped as her classmates and teachers cheered.

The house was beautifully decorated with colorful balloons, confetti was everywhere, and there was a huge banner that read "Congratulations, Lily, you did it!"

"But Dad, I didn't really do anything. Nothing's changed yet."

"Are you kidding me? You planted a seed. One that will grow and turn into something beautiful and amazing. Without you, they would have never thought to form a special committee to stop testing on animals."

Her dad looked at her with eyes that couldn't be more serious. "As IF nothing has changed yet! Lily, you ARE the change!"

Lily spent the rest of the day talking to her friends about Berlin and the animals on the grounds and wondered what kind of role she now had; Speaker for the Animals, it sounded good anyway.

After everyone left, Lily retired upstairs to unpack and relax before going to bed. It was still a school night, and she needed a little rest.

But not before talking to Ralph. "I wish I could give you a big hug. I am so happy for you and proud of you."

"Actually, I was so scared they weren't going to listen to me and then just escort me out. And just think, I wanted to quit! How stupid would that have been? What would have happened then? Nothing!"

She opened the balcony door to let in some fresh air. The full moon shone brightly through her thin curtains.

Lily turned around to finish unpacking.

Plunk! A sound from her balcony could only mean one guest.

"I am so proud of you!" Alo said as he gingerly walked inside.

They spent the next hour talking about her visit to Berlin and laughing about everyone's reaction to seeing all those animals. And about her two odd dreams with him apparently not really chasing her but playing games.

"Can you promise me you won't scare me in my dreams like that again?"

"I can only promise something I have control over, but to me, it sounded like you were just scared about school and your presentation, not me."

"Either way, I'm kinda glad it's over," Lily confessed.

"It's not over though. This the beginning of something beautiful. Something amazing, and I hope you can feel it, too."

"I guess I can feel it," Lily said, unsure of what he meant, but too tired to ask.

"I will now leave you. You had a busy week and need rest. We can talk another day," Alo said and slowly walked to the balcony and jumped off without a sound.

Awoken by a bright light, Lily squinted. "Is that you, Mother Nature?"

"Yes, I had to see you tonight and give you this." Mother Nature handed her a beautiful white lily. "The white lily means life, innocence, and purity. I have been nurturing this flower for you for ten years, waiting for this very moment to give it to you. It is your flower, Lily. It will protect you forever."

Mother Nature magically waved her hand, and a beautiful crystal vase with water appeared on Lily's desk.

"Come into the forest with your friends tomorrow after school. I have a surprise for all of you," Mother Nature said and disappeared, leaving an ascending white sparkle shower in her place.

With a huge smile on her face, Lily fell asleep.

The next day at school was extraordinary. Again, Lily felt like a rock star, but she only enjoyed it a short time. She was relieved when the teacher came in to restore peace and order again.

The entire school met in the auditorium to present Lily with another award for her success in Berlin. She was also asked to be the Vice-President of the Conscious Students Club, a student-led group that helped faculty make conscious decisions relating to the school curriculum, book purchases, and student activities. She felt honored and agreed without hesitation.

The auditorium was dismissed, and class resumed. On her way down the hall, Lily almost ran right into Viktoria, who was going the other way.

"Oh, well, look who's here, Miss Bigshot! You don't fool me, Missy. I know you're not perfect and I'm gonna prove it some-day!" Viktoria nudged past her.

Whatever. Lily tried not to get upset over her, but she still worried. Lily didn't like enemies with a cause.

The day passed by quickly, and before she knew it, she, Eva, and Till were walking into the woods to meet Mother Nature.

At their normal meeting spot, they didn't see her. Instead, hundreds of animals, big and small, weak and strong, greeted them with cheers. Lily told them about the trip, then Mother Nature appeared.

She seemed larger than ever before, and her bright, green cat's eyes sparkled like emeralds.

In one big swooping motion, Mother Nature opened her wings as far as they could reach. The feathers were still sparse and not in full plumage, but that's not what surprised Lily. Golden, sparkly light shone from each feather, and she looked more beautiful than ever before. She looked healthy!

"How could this happen? I didn't save any animals yet!" Lily asked.

"But you did, Lily. After your speech, a few government officials made some calls to get the ball rolling," Mother Nature said. "One call they made was to Dr. Schwarz, the lab director you visited. He immediately stopped all testing and told his staff to take care of the animals as best they could until the rehabilitation team arrived. His entire staff took off their white lab coats and comforted every animal in that building, all weekend long. They took shifts. Dr. Schwarz never left the building and cared for the monkeys himself!

"He contacted the best rehab facility in all of Europe and flew in an expert team early this morning. They have arranged for their rehabilitation to start tomorrow!" Mother Nature gleamed with joy.

"You saved at least 300 lab animals already, and those new feathers are starting to grow."

Lily couldn't believe her ears. She ran up to Mother Nature and gave her the biggest hug ever.

"I thank you with all my heart, and so does every animal on this planet. You are a legend, dear Lily, and we are forever grateful for you. But, there is more work to be done. This is just the beginning. Are you willing to continue to help us?"

"Of course, what do you want me to do?" Lily eagerly asked.

"Go home and rest. Enjoy this wonderful holiday season and spend time outside in nature and in front of the fireplace with your family and friends. We'll meet again real soon," Mother Nature said and vanished, but this time, she left a trail of white lilies and green sparkles in her place.

Feeling on top of the world, Lily, Eva, and Till walked home after celebrating with the forest animals. Hand in hand, they skipped through the woods past Marley, the maple tree, went through the small clearing, sidled down the slippery, muddy hill, swung around the big spruce tree, and wiggled through the thick bushes to enter Lily's backyard.

The End

MOTHER NATURE

FIFTEEN SIMPLE THINGS TO HELP SAVE (LAB) ANIMALS

Saving animals may seem like a huge task, but if you break it down into simple tasks, you can accomplish a lot with little effort. Here are a few things you can easily do from home, with or without the help of your parents.

1. Only purchase cruelty-free products such as cosmetics, body care and household products. Check for valid cruelty-free symbols and these websites to make sure. Remember, the claim 'we're against testing on animals' means nothing.

Leaping Bunny List

PETA List

BDIH (German Association - badge below)

2. If you're not sure if your favorite products are cruelty-free, please write the company and ask them these three questions:

a. Are any of your end products, raw materials, or ingredients tested on animals?

b. Do any 3rd parties test on animals on your behalf?

c. Do you sell your products in China, outside of Hong Kong*?

* The Chinese government requires – or at least used to

require – foreign cosmetic brands sold in China to be tested on animals. This law, however, does/did not apply to cosmetics sold in Hong Kong, nor to online products. There are more rules and loopholes to the Chinese law which make it confusing for those not working in this industry. For more information, read this blog post from Ethical Elephant: https://ethicalelephant.com/understanding-china-animal-testing-laws.

3. Contact your government officials to inspire them to take a stand against animal testing. You can start by asking their opinion about animal testing and ask questions about the current law in your country and if any measures are being taken to introduce alternative methods.

4. Get involved with a local or national animal rights organization that is active in the ban of animal testing.

5. Talk to your friends and family. Education is key and you may find that many people just don't know that there are better alternatives to animal testing (the so-called NAMs you read about in this book). Now that you know this information, you can speak for the animals to try to inspire others to buy cruelty-free products.

6. Talk openly to your teacher in biology about classroom dissection. I'll never forget my horrifying experience as a young student. Luckily, many students are no longer forced to cut open dead animals if they don't want to.

7. When you're old enough, you can sign up to donate your organs and leave your body for science because human bodies can help humans more than any other species.

8. Follow cruelty-free and animal rights influencers (bloggers, youtubers) and don't shy away from asking questions and engaging with them on a higher level than just liking their video/blog post. Here are a few to keep an eye on:

Logical Harmony (logicalharmony.net)
Ethical Elephant (ethicalelephant.com)
Cruelty-Free Kitty (crueltyfreekitty.com)
The Little Foxes (thelilfoxes.com)
Phyrra (phyrra.net)
My Beauty Bunny (beautybunny.com)

9. Celebrate *World Day for Laboratory Animals* on April 24th and any other international day that honors the rights of animals. You can see if any events are near your city or organize your own with your friends and neighbors.

10. Research organizations in your area (locally and nationally) that help laboratory animals and work with the government and labs to encourage a national ban on the testing of animals.

For example:

CAAT-Europe (Center for Alternatives to Animal Testing)
Founded in 2009, *CAAT-Europe* joint ventured with Johns Hopkins University in the USA and the University of Constance in Germany in 2010 to promote the development of new and improved methods in toxicology, to be a partner in strategy development, to provide platforms for different stakeholders, to exchange ideas, and to support the 3Rs (refinement, reduction, replacement) principle of humane science in different ways.

11. Set *ecosia.org* as your default search engine because they plant trees every time you search. Win-win!

12. If you or your parents are on social media, please connect with me because I often share information about other ways to help save animals.

Connect with me on these channels:
Instagram (instagram.com/jesslohmann)
Facebook (facebook.com/jesslohmann)
Twitter (twitter.com/jesslohm)
Pinterest (pinterest.com/jesslohm)
Website (jesslohmann.com)

13. Ask your parents to subscribe to my newsletter: *Talk About Nature!* for animal-saving and nature-related information as well as upcoming releases. The adventures of Lily Bowers have only just begun.
Subscribe here: (jesslohmann.com/subscribe).

14. Reviews are necessary to help spread the message and new readers to get an idea whether or not they want to spend the time reading a book. So, if you enjoyed this book, please ask your parents to write a review.

15. Ask your parents to join others in the *Raising Conscious Kids* group on Facebook (facebook.com/groups/raisingconsciouskids) to extend the conversation there as well.

Each small step you take to help protect animals is a step worth taking.

Mother Nature, the animals and I thank you for your contribution.

QUOTES THAT ROCK

"The greatness of a nation and its moral progress can be judged by the way its animals are treated."
  ~ Mahatma Gandhi

"The greatest danger to our future is apathy." "What you do makes a difference, and you have to decide what kind of difference you want to make."
  ~ Dr. Jane Goodall

"When the last tree has been cut down, the last fish caught, the last river poisoned, only then will we realize that one cannot eat money."
  ~ Alanis Obomsawin

"Until we stop harming all other living beings, we are still savages."
  ~ Thomas Jefferson

"And when they seek to oppress you and destroy you; rise and rise again and again like The Phoenix from the ashes; until the lambs have become lions and the rule of Darkness is no more."
  ~ Maitreya, The Friend of All Souls

All things are connected. Whatever befalls the earth befalls the sons of the earth. Man does not weave the web of life; he is merely a strand of it. Whatever he does to the web, he does to himself."
  ~ Ted Perry

"Every year tens of thousands of animals suffer and die in laboratory tests of cosmetics and household products...despite the fact that the test results do not help prevent or treat accidental or purposeful misuse of the products. Please join me in using your voice for those whose cries are forever sealed behind the laboratory doors."

~ Woody Harrelson

"Yesterday I was clever, so I wanted to change the world. Today I am wise, so I am changing myself."

~ Rumi

"Never doubt that a small group of thoughtful, committed citizens can change the world; indeed, it's the only thing that ever does."

~ Margaret Mead

"Empathy knows no country, no species, is universal and has always been available."

~ Harry Prosen

"The great lengths we go to help our animals is one thing that still sets us apart."

~ Laurel Braitman

"There will come a time when the world will look back to modern vivisection in the name of science, as they do now to burning at the stake in the name of religion."

~ Kathryn Bigelow

"All animals, human included, are equal and deserve love and respect."

~ Lily Bowers

"As soon as we're mindful about how we talk about animals, can we start to speak FOR the animals."

„As parents, we have the moral responsibility to keep the spirit of our children alive, healthy and happy. As humans, this extends to all living beings. Breaking the spirit of animals goes against the laws of nature and the universe."

~ Jess Lohmann

WORDS FROM THE WORLD

"We envisage a world in which every country enjoys sustained, inclusive and sustainable economic growth and decent work for all. One in which humanity lives in harmony with nature and in which wildlife and other living species are protected."
~ UN Sustainable Development Goals Political Declaration

The 17 Sustainable Development Goals (SDGs) were created by all 193 member states of the United Nations in 2015 to help improve the many global challenges we face today.

A 15-year plan was set to achieve all 17 goals. From combating poverty, to illiteracy, climate change and inequality to restoring biodiversity, clean water and sanitation, economic growth, affordable energy, etc.

Many achievements have been made, but the work in local and national governments is very slow and so it is our responsibility as caring individuals to step up and help out.

We, the people, have the power to reach these goals through our businesses, volunteering, giving back, spreading awareness, etc.

Since saving species is at the heart of Jess' mission, she's passionately committed to reaching these three goals:
    #13 Climate action
    #14: Life below water
    #15: Life on land

Because if we don't get these right, we — as a human animal species — will become extinct and then nothing else matters.

Nothing. Else. Matters.

ABOUT THE AUTHOR

Jess Lohmann envisions a kind world of healthy choices and opportunities for all animals, humans included.

One with no more child labor, sweatshops, animal abuse and testing, dangerous pandemics and harmful pesticides, GMOs and chemicals on the foods, clothes, meds and products we consume.

And a world without racism, intolerance, poverty and war.

Jess believes that if every human were to respect Mother Nature and all she takes care of, we would have world peace.

Because when we're one with nature, we're at peace with ourselves.

And when we're at peace with ourselves, we're at peace with others.

Does she believe in fairy dust? *Absolutely!*

But she also believes in the power of people and their ability to come together to change the world for the better.

Born and raised on Long Island, New York, Jess learned from her parents to **respect nature and all animals.**

She went on family camping trips, helped her mom care for and release rescued wild animals and worked as a vet's assistant and caretaker during high school and college.

In 1995, she moved to Germany and currently lives with her husband, daughter, dog and cat just a few blocks away from a forest rich with wildlife and spiritual beauty.

Not only does she enjoy writing, she also helps animal-saving visionary leaders create and implement an impactful ethical marketing strategy at Ethical Brand Marketing (ethicalbrandmarketing.com).

And because her voice is also in demand as a narrator, you can say **she markets, writes and speaks for the animals.**

Read more about Jess Lohmann on her website, jesslohmann.com, and sign up to her newsletter: **Talk about Nature!**

Photo Credit: Gabriele Protze, Bildnis Fotostudio

PROUD MEMBER OF

EARTH PROTECTORS

Mitglied im

S E N D — Social Entrepreneurship Netzwerk Deutschland

vd | s

Verband Deutscher Sprecher e.V.

1% FOR THE PLANET — MEMBER —

the ethical move.

The Alliance of Independent Authors — Author Member

ONE SHARED WORLD

WE SUPPORT THE GLOBAL GOALS — SUPPORTTHEGOALS.ORG

Ärzte gegen Tierversuche e.V.

E4F

OFFICIAL ETHICAL INFLUENCERS MEMBER

Meaningful Business 100

#ethical HOUR TRIBE MEMBER

Printed in Poland
by Amazon Fulfillment
Poland Sp. z o.o., Wrocław

63725987R00106